aHunter4Gotten

By

Cynthia A Clement

Text copyright © 2016 Cynthia A Clement

Print Edition
ISBN: 978-1-988019-17-8

Cover designed by RomCon®
www.romcon.com
Cover Image: Period Images,
www.periodimages.com

Dedication

To Maria
May all your writing dreams and personal aspirations come true.

A special thanks to Jan Carol Abney, Kim Barrows, and John for editing, proofreading, and inspiration.

Chapter 1

Chaos surrounded him.

They'd crashed and somehow he'd survived.

Twisted metal littered the ground, and the odor of burning flesh permeated the air. Flames from the spacecraft that had brought them to this planet, reached high into the sky and broke the darkness of night. One of the mission leaders pulled him to a large contorted box of wreckage and commanded him to stay. Another survivor, Catal, joined him. The two of them were decoys while the rest of the unit escaped.

Their commanders ordered them not to resist arrest.

He and Catal were left as bait.

The steady breathing and beating of Eogan's heart marked the passage of time as he waited for his fate. Within an hour, a helicopter's light illuminated the night and caught him in its beam. He readied himself for battle. Men jumped out of the aircraft, and the crunch of their boots on the debris-filled ground sounded like death approaching. Adrenaline rushed through his body and he knew with a certainty that he could defeat these men and escape. He had only one problem.

Orders had to be obeyed.

There was honor in giving his life for his fellow brothers. He would die knowing they would be safe. Whatever his future, he had upheld the Sacred Code that all warriors lived by. It was reward enough for a Hunter.

Someone grabbed his arm.

"Mission time."

The command shattered through his nightmare. The sharp voice of his handler pierced through his sleep.

Eogan shook off the lingering tentacles of the recurring dream that haunted him every night. It was the last moment of freedom he'd known. The moment his destiny had changed. He'd gone from a warrior, honored and respected, to a killing machine, forced to obey the orders of human and Albireon conspirators. He looked up at the man scowling down at him. A pistol was aimed at his head.

General Carter.

A man obsessed with violence and power.

Carter was of average height, barrel chested with a large neck and steely gray eyes. His cropped hair was salt and pepper, and the frown-lines on his forehead suggested his age to be mid-forties. He was the last in a long line of humans who'd used and abused Eogan since his capture thirty years ago.

"They're ready to trust you with an assignment." The general's voice was harsh as he waved the gun at him. "Don't screw up. You're still on probation."

Eogan had been under lock down at the Pine Gap facility in Australia for almost six months. He'd helped a fellow Hunter, Partlan, and the woman he was with, Grace, escape. His handlers couldn't prove that he'd aided them, but they hadn't been willing to take any chances. They'd thrown him into isolation in a cell on the lowest level of the underground military base. Even with implants and chemical restraints, Eogan was capable of destroying them before they would have a chance to terminate him. This new assignment must be too dangerous for them to risk sending one of their own men.

He sat and stretched his arms above his head.

Anticipation flowed through his veins.

Most of his life had been spent on Earth even though he was originally from the planet Cygnus. He was a Hunter. Hunters were an elite warrior race bred to obey the Kaladin who ruled Cygnus. He was also clan Rioge, which meant he was genetically modified and trained to lead men. Since crash-landing on this planet when he was fifteen, he'd been coerced into following the orders of his human handlers.

For thirty years he had obeyed them.

No more.

Their lies had been exposed. He was not alone on this planet. Other Hunters had survived and he intended to find his brother warriors. The humans who used him were allied with an alien race known as the Albireons. The Albireons had seduced his handlers with promises of technological advances and power. Little did the humans realize that the Albireons had no intention of keeping their word. It was all lies. Once the Albireons had what they needed, they would kill every human on this planet. No one would survive.

"When do I leave?" Eogan kept his voice neutral. He didn't want to give Carter a reason to suspect his real motive until it was too late.

"Immediately." General Carter stood back and straightened his green military jacket. "There is a helicopter waiting above ground to take you to the plane. You'll be briefed about the mission en route."

Eogan nodded. "Will you be accompanying me?"

"No. I can't be connected to this operation. If you're caught, no one will rescue you."

"Understood."

Eogan pushed aside his regret that Carter wasn't coming with him. He'd kept sane these past six months in isolation by envisioning exacting justice on the general. The man had no ethics and had broken the Sacred Code numerous times. There was only one recourse for a man such as General Carter.

Death.

For ten years he'd done the bidding of this cruel and sadistic man. A man who took pleasure in causing pain, and delighted in exerting his power over others. He was a poor excuse for a human. Honor demanded that Eogan kill the general. If he'd been going on the mission to supervise, it would have been easy to do. Now, he would have to wait for another time.

He pulled on a tee-shirt before sitting down to tie up his boots. It was the same as every other sortie he'd been sent on. No one would be there to protect or rescue him. He was disposable. If caught, they would terminate him rather than take the chance of him talking. They could not risk exposure of their secret organization even if it meant the destruction of a valuable weapon.

Eogan would never break protocol.

A warrior didn't expose his mission, under any circumstance.

They had spent years trying to make him disclose details about his unit when he'd first been captured. He had withstood their torture and abuse. He hadn't given out any information on the others who had survived the crash. He lived by the code that all Hunters followed and he hadn't broken his vow. He was clan Rioge; a leader of men. He would never disgrace himself or betray his brothers.

He stood and shrugged into his camo field-vest. He towered over the general by a good foot and Carter jumped back. He kept his pistol trained on Eogan. There was a flicker of panic in the general's eyes, but it was gone a second later. He was used to this reaction, not only with Carter, but also with the other men he was deployed with. The humans used him to do their killing, but his reputation as a skilled warrior meant they feared him also.

"Any special instructions?"

"Your mission supervisor will give you the details." The general moved back and signaled for the cell door to be opened. "Remember, one false step, and you'll be eliminated."

Eogan nodded. He had two implants. One monitored and controlled him, the other was set to self-destruct once the command was initiated. He would only have a couple of hours to remove them before headquarters realized the assignment had gone wrong. It was a slight window, but possible. He'd been planning his escape for the past six months. He was ready.

Once he fled, there would be no turning back.

He followed the general through the maze of dank underground tunnels and up the elevator to the surface. There was a helicopter and several soldiers waiting for them. Eogan jumped into the copter and strapped himself in. He was unarmed. There would be no opportunity to overpower his guards until they landed at their destination. His best opportunity to escape would be once he was on the ground and knew his mission. For now, he would sit back, assess the weakness of his opponents, and plan his course of action.

He arrived, eighteen hours and several aircraft changes later, in the darkened terrain of a Middle Eastern country. He joined the mission team minutes before they all boarded the stealth helicopter that flew them on the last leg of their journey. It took a few seconds for Eogan to acclimatize to the hot humid air once they had disembarked on the ground. The night was cooler than daytime, and that was probably why they were going in now. They also had the cover of dark to hide their activities. It was a moonless night.

"Listen up."

The team leader gathered his soldiers around. There were ten in total.

They left Eogan standing by the helicopter. As usual, they didn't want him to know anything about the mission until it was time for him to kill. When they were upon the target he would be given instructions. Explanations were not necessary for him because his handlers considered him less than human. He was an alien who had no feelings or purpose. He mattered only as a weapon.

Eogan was familiar with their secrecy.

They never trusted him and for the first time they had a reason not to. He would neither hinder nor help their mission. They would be on their own. Escape and freedom were his goals and the sooner he accomplished that, the better.

The team leader approached Eogan when he was finished with his instructions. He was young in years, yet his alertness and command of the men suggested he was a well-seasoned soldier. Eogan had been studying him since he'd first sat across from him on the helicopter. His epaulet announced his rank as captain and his name-tag said Barton. He was about six feet tall, with short-cropped, dark hair, and blue eyes that skittered away from Eogan.

Barton stared at the western horizon.

"I understand you do the killing." The man cleared his throat. "I've always worked as a team in the past."

"That is usually best." Eogan's respect for the man grew. "It's your mission, so the decision is yours."

"I would prefer to let my men go in first."

"Understood."

"If there's a problem then you can help."

"Do I get a weapon?" Eogan didn't need one to escape, but it would be easier.

"No." The captain shook his head. "My orders are very clear about that. My superiors said that you would be able to fight even without a weapon."

A prickling unease skipped across the back of Eogan's neck. His stomach tensed as his sense of danger was triggered. Something was wrong with this mission, but there was no time to examine it further. This was his only chance if he was going to escape.

"Can you tell me where we are?"

"Turkey. We're on the southern border at Akcakale. It's close to Kobani, Syria."

It was an area of civil war and turmoil. Eogan was familiar with the region. He'd been deployed on more than one operation here, and could only guess what the real purpose of this sortie was. If the Albireons controlled the district, then they were in favor of the unrest and wanted to accelerate it. A planet at war and living in fear was easier to dominate than one at peace. It was a classic stratagem taken from centuries of planetary conquest. It was effective and used often.

"Do you want me to cross the border with you?" Eogan had no doubt that the mission was in Syria.

"Yes." The soldier shifted on his feet. "You are to come with us and then wait for further commands."

He straightened his shoulders and moved away from the helicopter. "As you wish."

Barton put his hand up to stop him. "I don't know what we're going to encounter once we cross into Syria, but I won't let you face it unarmed."

"You are a man of integrity."

Eogan joined the others and followed them as they started their covert march to the beleaguered city. The helicopter took off as soon as they crossed into Syria. That meant no hope of a speedy rescue. These men would either die here, or have to find their own way home.

It was callous and without honor, yet that was how the shadow government operated. The organization was comprised of humans whose sole function was to protect the Albireons. They couldn't risk others finding out about the deals they had made with the extraterrestrials. It might expose the lies they'd told to hide their real agenda; which was to control the planet.

They moved with a stealth and silence that only years of training and conditioning could hone. These men were experienced soldiers, hired because of their skills. Whatever the reasons for them being here, they had been chosen because they were an elite unit. Eogan questioned why he was needed. Something about this mission triggered his defensive instincts. All was not as it seemed.

The attack came with speed and surprise.

They'd walked into an ambush.

Chapter 2

They were caught in a narrow, man-made corridor of vehicles and buildings. There was no escape in front of them and when they turned to retreat, their exit was blocked also. Guns flared and grenades exploded around them. They were outnumbered and overpowered. Their presence had been anticipated and the only thing they could do now was fight for survival.

If they lived through this, they might be able to complete their mission. Eogan suspected the mission was bogus. This elite unit had been sent into a well-planned trap so that they could be slaughtered. The question was why kill the members of this squad in such a clandestine fashion? The only reasonable explanation was that these men were suspected traitors and Carter wanted that possibility buried. The best way to do that was to have them die in battle.

The fact that he was here, meant they were suspicious of him too.

He'd been marked for termination.

Eogan stayed in the rear as instructed. The moment the first grenade exploded, Barton handed him a pistol and then ran to the front of the line to lead his men. Eogan dropped to the ground and checked his weapon. He had only one round of bullets, so he'd have to make certain each one hit its mark. After that, it would be hand-to-hand combat.

A team member was shot in front of him.

Eogan crawled to the downed soldier.

There were no signs of life. He picked up the abandoned assault rifle, rolled behind the wheels of a burnt out pickup truck, and took aim. Staying to fight would lessen his chances of survival, but he was a soldier. Honor demanded that he help. His eyes had adjusted to the dark and his shots hit their marks. When the area was cleared he moved forward with the team.

He sought cover behind building debris and abandoned vehicles. He kept hidden, shooting and killing their attackers. As soon as he killed one of the enemy, three more would take their place. The acrid smell of spent ammunition filled the night air and the loud retort of guns being fired continued in shattering repetition. The attack was relentless.

The odds against them were enormous.

The team members were being slaughtered.

If the complete decimation of the unit had been the mission objective, then it had been successful. Eogan didn't have time to ponder why these men had been targeted for elimination. A couple of the men were still firing their weapons in the distance. Soon, they became silent too. Now was his opportunity to escape and he turned his gun to the enemy who were blocking his retreat. He took aim and started shooting. His targets went down.

He turned and crawled toward the direction they had entered from. He took weapons from the team members he found, along with their name patches. These soldiers deserved to be remembered. It didn't matter that they fought for an organization that was corrupt and wanted to see humanity destroyed. They had died in battle.

He killed the last attacker and pulled the body into an abandoned building. He stripped off his own jacket and shirt before grabbing the military vest off the dead soldier and rifling through its contents. There were some emergency food packs, ammo, a flashlight, and a short-bladed knife.

The knife was perfect.

He had to remove the first implant.

It was in his forearm and had been inserted at birth. This device was how the Kaladin on his home planet had modified and enhanced his physical capabilities. The Albireons and their human allies had been using it to follow and monitor him since he'd been captured. Now was the time to get rid of it.

He took the knife and in the narrow beam of the flashlight, he cut into his left forearm and dug out the tiny device. There was a small trickle of blood that he wiped away with the back of his hand. He ripped a long strip of material from the bottom of his shirt and wrapped it around the incision and his forearm. Experience had taught him that the wound would be healed within hours. That was one of the benefits of this planet.

He didn't feel any immediate change in his body. Knowing that he was no longer controlled by outside forces sent a surge of relief through him. He was in charge of his own fate for the first time in his life.

His destiny was with his fellow Hunters.

Time was important if he was going to escape.

He placed his implant into the pocket of the dead man's pants. The man was shorter than he, so he couldn't exchange clothing with him. He put his shirt and jacket back on. There was no ammunition left, so the guns were useless for protection. He would rely on the confusion of the battlefield to mask the truth of his desertion. He didn't want the Albireon security forces to know he was still alive until he could get the main implant in his neck removed.

He kept low as he hugged the building and moved away from the fighting and back to the border. He had no bullets left so he threw his weapons away and made a dash for safety. He could have stayed and fought until the last man was dead, but he had no reason to.

His only goal was escape.

The details of the attack suggested that the ambush had been set up to guarantee that no one survived. They expected him to be killed along with the others. The odds were too great for anyone to survive. It wasn't the first time the Albireons had underestimated the fighting expertise of a Hunter.

He hiked west and headed for the road once he crossed the border into Turkey. The nearest city was Sanliurfa. It had an airport and he might be able to get a vehicle. His chances of escape decreased the longer he traveled by foot. He reached a high point of ground and stopped to survey the area behind him. The guns were silent and he could see the glow of a giant fire.

They were burning the evidence.

They didn't want anything left in case there was an official inquiry.

They would assume that he was killed with the rest of the men. His freedom wouldn't last long, though. Daylight would bring in another team to assess the situation from the ground and that would expose the truth of his desertion. At most, he had five hours before they suspected he was still alive. The destruction of the one implant and the possible tracking devices in his clothing would confuse them.

They would only access the implant in his neck if they suspected he was alive. A signal would be sent from his handlers in Australia to confirm he lived. He needed to remove and destroy it as soon as possible. Otherwise, they would know that he'd survived and would trigger the self-destruct mechanism. The location of the last implant meant he needed help with its removal. He needed to find his fellow Hunters quickly.

He located the road and started toward the lights on the horizon. It would take at least an hour to reach the city and that was going at a steady jog. He focused on survival as he let the rhythm of his boots stomping on the packed surface of the roadway guide his journey. Dwelling on what he couldn't change was useless. If death found him this night, so be it. At least he would die a free man.

When he reached the outskirts of Sanliurfa, he took a side road that went around the city. He couldn't risk surveillance cameras finding him before he reached the airport. By then, it would be too late for them to react to his escape. Once he was out of Turkey, he'd have help from his fellow Hunters.

He jogged north when a loud cracking noise stopped him.

Someone had fired a pistol.

He turned in the direction of the blast. No other sound reached him. He continued forward when a woman's scream ripped through the silence. Her shriek was filled with fear and terror.

Eogan halted.

He couldn't leave a woman in distress. It was against every tenet of the Sacred Code. His eyes scanned the horizon looking for some indication of where the noise had come from. A slight flicker of light reflected off an object. He edged nearer to the light when the scream came again. It came from the same spot where he'd seen the light. He increased his pace.

The blast of a gun ripped through the night again. He stopped and waited. The woman shouted again. This time he could make out her words.

"You killed him."

The next sound was men's voices talking in a language he didn't recognize. Laughter followed and their tone was enough to let him know that the woman would be next. Time was of the essence if he was going to save her.

He ran.

He found them in a dip of earth off the main roadway. The lights of a jeep were trained on a group of men surrounding a woman. Six men in total were laughing and poking at her as she tried to stay out of reach of their hands. Outrage filled him. No man should disrespect a woman, much less terrorize her. They violated every law that Eogan had been bred to obey. He had no other option but to exact justice.

The Sacred Code was very clear about the penalty for hurting a woman.

These men must die.

He searched for a weapon to use. There were three dead bodies on the ground, but none of them were armed. Eogan clenched his hands and eased his breathing. He would have to kill some of the men with his bare hands. Silence and surprise, were his best strategy until he was closer to the woman. Eogan crouched and edged forward. He used the cover of the jeep to sneak up to the first man.

He grabbed him around the neck, covered his mouth, and twisted.

The crunch of breaking bones was masked by the laughter from the others.

Eogan eased the dead body to the ground before moving to the next man. He killed him in the same manner. This time, the sound of the body dropping to the ground alerted the rest of the group to an intruder. Eogan reached the third man just as a shot was fired. He spun around so that the bullet hit the man he was holding. He used the dead man's body as a shield as he rushed toward the shooter.

Bullets whizzed past him.

Eogan reached the shooter and clutched his hand and gun.

He twisted the weapon backwards just as the next shot rang out.

The man slumped to the ground. Eogan dropped the body he'd been using as a shield and grabbed the gun. He fired in quick succession killing the last two men before either was able to aim their weapons.

He glanced around the area to be certain everything was safe. The woman he had rescued was standing in the headlights. Her hands were clenched at her sides and she was staring down at one of the dead men. She was short and plump, wearing jeans and a hip-length jacket. She had heavy-rimmed glasses, but the rest of her face was covered by strands of hair that had fallen out of her ponytail.

He had the urge to gather her into his arms and assure her that she was safe.

He pushed the impulse away.

He was a Hunter and women were forbidden. He took a deep breath. Escape was his goal, and he had to focus on the best way to do that. He went to one of the dead men and picked up his gun. He wasn't certain what was ahead, but facing it armed would be easier. He turned to walk away when the woman yelled.

"You can't leave me here."

Chapter 3

Hester's father had always said that her curiosity would get her killed one day, and he was right. Seconds ago, she'd been in danger of being raped and murdered. Now, she was staring at the man who had just walked into the group of thugs and eliminated all of them. He gave her a quick glance and then turned back toward the road.

She could see her rescuer in the jeep's headlights. He was tall and very muscular if the tightness of his clothes were any indication. The ease and skill he'd used to dispatch those men had been frightening, but he hadn't touched her. His actions had saved her life, and right now she was out of options. She had to trust him. She was alone and defenseless.

She couldn't stay on this isolated road.

It was a crazy position to be caught in, especially in a country where women were still expected to live by very conservative values. She wouldn't last an hour, much less long enough to find the airport and leave this place.

"Take me with you."

"A warrior does not associate with women." His deep voice echoed through her body. A shiver went through her at the coldness of his words as he turned back to the road.

"You just saved me from death." Her voice sounded desperate, but she couldn't stop the fear that was coursing through her. "At least take me to the airport."

The man stopped and pointed to the jeep. "Is that your vehicle?"

"No. Those creeps came in it." Hester trembled as she remembered the moment the men had prevented their escape and then surrounded them. "Two of the other guys I came here with, took off in our van."

"They had no honor if they left you here to die."

"That was the least of their downfalls."

Hester's teeth chattered and she rubbed her arms to try and ease the aftereffects of fear that still coursed through her body. The first chance Steve and Franklin had, they'd reversed the van and raced away from the jeep that had blocked them. There hadn't been a backward glance for her or the others who were left on the roadside.

"Why are you here?"

"I'm an archaeologist and I was trying to explore Gobekli Tepe."

She glanced behind her shoulder. It had been a crazy idea to visit the site at night. She'd known it the first time Steve had suggested it, but she couldn't resist the lure of exploring some of the pillar markings up close and without supervision. She'd thrown logic and commonsense out the window and had eagerly agreed to join their expedition.

"Would it not be easier to view in daylight?"

Hester could almost see the lift of his eyebrows at how ridiculous her plan sounded.

"They said that we wouldn't be able to get near enough." She swallowed back her nausea. "Now the others will never see it."

"It was foolish to travel with men who could not defend you." The man's voice held no sympathy.

"We didn't expect to be attacked." Hester's voice rose in defense. "It's not like I woke up this morning and decided that a gang of thugs was going to stop our vehicle and kill us."

"Why?"

Hester frowned. "Why didn't we plan to be ambushed?"

"Why did they force you off the road?" The man turned to her and crossed his arms over his massive chest. "Were you doing something that made you look suspicious?"

"Samuel said it would be fun to drive beside the road. He thought we might be able to pick up some artifacts."

"That doesn't sound legal."

Hester's face flushed.

Thankfully it was dark. Her rescuer didn't need to know how embarrassed she'd been at the antics of the guys that she'd hitched a ride with. It had been a mistake from the moment she'd jumped into the van. They were Ufologists and told her that they'd been to Gobekli Tepe before. They hadn't mentioned that they liked to break the law.

"It isn't." Hester's voice cracked. "I didn't know they were going to do it."

"Where did these other men come from?"

Hester shook her head. "One moment I was trying to jump back into the van, and the next, these bright lights were blocking our way.

They just appeared."

The man took a couple of steps closer. "They were waiting?"

"It seemed like it." She bent down and picked up her leather backpack. The men had taken it from her and tossed it around so that she couldn't reach it. Her stomach clenched at how helpless she'd been. It had been reminiscent of recess in grade school when the other kids had relentlessly teased and bullied her. She'd thought she'd put those memories behind her long ago.

"There is no reason for a vehicle to be waiting here. It is not a well-traveled road and is far from the city."

"You're forgetting the ruins." Hester didn't hide her awe. "I've wanted to explore the stones since I learned about it in undergraduate school."

"It seems you did not choose the right time." The man crouched over a body.

"I thought visiting the site with fellow enthusiasts would be the best way." Hester knelt on the ground and then leaned back against her feet. "They said they'd been here before and never had a problem. They come here frequently to look at the carvings and search the skies for UFO's."

The man looked up at her. "You were looking for these objects too?"

"No." Hester opened her pack and pulled out a bottle of water. "It's not that I don't believe, because I do. I just wanted to see the Gobekli Tepe engravings up close. I don't think that they're remnants of a temple like the current academics believe."

"What do you think they are?"

"Evidence of Ancient Aliens."

There was a long pause before the man spoke. "That doesn't seem to be a reasonable belief given the fact that you said you were an archaeologist."

"Exactly." She twisted the lid off the bottle. "Now you know why I was willing to go with those guys."

"You were here in secret." The man stood and walked over to one of the other bodies. "These men are military."

"Turkish?" Hester took a sip of the cool liquid.

He shook his head. "European or American."

Hester choked and spit her water on the ground. "Why would the United States Armed Forces be interested in a bunch of UFO enthusiasts? Unless this means aliens are on Earth."

"Soldiers in an allied country is hardly evidence of aliens on the planet." His voice was dry. "We need to leave before their commander wonders why they're not communicating with him."

She stood. "So you'll take me with you. Great. I'm Hester Adams by the way." She held her hand out to him.

He looked down at her hand and then up at her. "I am Eogan."

Her arm dropped to her side. Men usually ignored her, but they didn't go out of their way to be rude. He'd saved her life so she would forgive his behavior. Before she had a chance to say anything else, Eogan sat on the ground and unlaced his boots. He went over to one of the dead men and measured his foot against his. Then he pulled off his shirt and jacket and stripped out of his pants and underwear.

Hester's eyes widened. She'd seen nude men in magazines before, but never in real life, and never anything as wonderfully fit as Eogan. He was spectacular. He was also unaware of her scrutiny. With a gasp, she remembered her manners and turned around.

"Are you hurt?" Eogan asked.

Hester shook her head. "I'm giving you privacy to change."

"That is not necessary." Eogan's voice was low. "I'm used to being watched."

"By lots of women I bet." The words were out of her mouth before she could stop them.

"No." His voice sounded puzzled. "Why does it matter who watches?"

"I shouldn't have assumed that you were heterosexual." She wished the ground would drop away and bury her. She hadn't felt this foolish in years. Just because he was a hunk didn't mean he preferred ladies. "You'll have to forgive me. I talk too much when I'm nervous."

There was a loud banging.

Hester turned around to see Eogan beating his clothes with a giant stone.

"Is there an insect on it?"

"Possibly a tracking device." He slammed the rock down on his boots. "I don't want to risk them finding me too soon."

"Are you in trouble?" Hester's words were hesitant. "I hope stopping to help me didn't make it worse?"

"It is my duty to protect women and children. Only a man with no honor would have walked away."

"Thank you for rescuing me." Hester knew that she was babbling, but she didn't want Eogan to leave without her telling him that she was grateful he'd saved her life. "Those men did not intend to let me live."

"No." Eogan buttoned the shirt he'd taken from one of the dead men. "They had no honor."

"I don't want to think about their intentions." She shivered. The paralyzing fear of knowing that they had intended to rape and kill her would linger in her psyche for days.

"I must go." He turned.

"You can't leave me out here." Hester ran up beside him. "At least take me to Sanliurfa."

"It would be dangerous for you to be with me." He motioned behind him. "I believe those men were waiting for me, not you. You and your friends were only a diversion."

"What if others like them are out here?" Hester shuddered. "I'll be safer with you."

There was a few seconds of silence before he replied, "True."

Eogan went to the jeep and shut the lights off. Darkness enveloped them. The only illumination came from the stars in the sky. He climbed behind the wheel and paused. He seemed to be debating whether to let her join him, when she noticed a bright light in the distance. She squinted her eyes and adjusted her glasses higher on her nose as she tried to make out what was headed toward them.

Eogan turned in the direction of her gaze.

He gave a low growl and pointed to the passenger door. "Jump in."

Hester didn't wait to be told twice. She ran around to the other side and climbed into the jeep. She wanted to get as far away as possible if others were coming. The problem was they were blocking the way to Sanliurfa. There was only one direction for them to go and that was toward the ruins.

Eogan twisted the key in the ignition and drove the vehicle away from the town. He avoided the road and kept the headlights off as he sped off.

"I hope you're familiar with this ruin of yours because we're going to hide there."

Hester hung onto the side of the jeep as it rocked over the rough terrain. "We won't have a problem finding a safe place. I've only seen pictures and videos, but it's a large area with some covering."

"Good. Those men are aiming straight for us."

Chapter 4

They drove in silence for several minutes.

Hester's anxiety rose with each passing second. Her nerves were frayed and the quiet was making it worse. "Doesn't it bother you that people are following you?"

"It is better than letting them kill us."

Hester shivered at the cold chill of his voice. "You act as if this were an everyday occurrence."

"I am a warrior."

"So that makes it all right to have people stalk you?" She shook her head. "The closest I've ever come to danger before this, was trying to drive on the freeway."

"You're a woman. You are not meant to fight."

"Are you suggesting that women can't do what men do?" Hester fought to keep her voice civil as she glared at him. "You sound like a chauvinist."

"I don't understand your words. I do battle so others can be safe." Eogan's voice was filled with confusion. "Would you rather that I had let those men murder you?"

Hester crossed her arms. "That's not what I meant. You inferred that a woman wasn't able to take care of herself."

"Women command and men obey." His tone was serious. "I was bred and trained to protect."

She strained her eyes in the dark to see whether he was joking. He was focused on the terrain ahead and all she could see was the side of his face. He had sounded sincere though.

"If that's the case, why didn't you take me with you when I first asked?" Hester pursed her lips together. "You were going to leave me there unprotected."

"I was trying to keep you alive and unharmed." Eogan glanced at her. "It's unsafe for you to be around me."

Hester stared out the window. "It can't be worse than being attacked by those men."

"You are upset because of your friends' deaths." Eogan steered the vehicle onto the road. "I apologize."

"It was a horrible thing to see." Hester shuddered. "Josh had been so nice inviting me to go along with them. I'm glad Steve and Franklin were able to get away. Steve's been traveling in Turkey for years. He's the real expert. Franklin didn't say much, so I'm not sure what his area of knowledge is."

"It is my fault they are dead." Eogan pressed down on the accelerator and the car jerked forward. "They were waiting for me."

"If they wanted you, why did they stop us?"

He looked at her. In the dim light of the dashboard she could see that his eyes were narrowed. "I have found that men like them do not have honor."

"All I wanted was to see Gobekli Tepe." Hester clutched her bag closer to her body. "When the Germans, who are in charge of the excavation, refused to let me on the site in a professional capacity, I decided to go on my own."

"Would not another archaeologist have been useful?"

"I suppose they didn't think my position at the university, or the sites I've worked at in North America, was enough experience."

That wasn't the only reason they didn't want her onboard. She had asked if she could help in secret. She didn't want the school she taught at knowing about her work at Gobekli Tepe. That had probably sent up red flags.

"Do you spend all of your time at these archaeological sites?" Eogan swerved off the road again and drove in a straight line to what resembled a row of covered tents.

"Most of my time is spent in the classroom." She didn't have anything to be ashamed of, but it felt anticlimactic to admit that she had limited field experience. After tonight's incident she doubted she'd venture out alone again.

"You teach." His voice held approval. "That is a noble thing to do."

A flicker of pride filled her chest. "I always thought so, but sometimes you want to see things for yourself. I've read so much about Gobekli Tepe in books, and I've seen pictures. I wanted to examine it up close."

"You think it will be different than the images?" Eogan slowed the vehicle.

"I think that the depictions we're allowed to see don't tell the whole truth." Hester's tone was dry. "I'm not naïve. I know academics hold back information so they can be the first to publish. In this case, I don't think they understand the significance of what they've discovered."

"What is that?"

"I think it's evidence that aliens once visited this planet." Hester lowered her voice as she uttered the heresy. If another archaeologist heard her, it would be the end of her career as a respected scientist.

"You can tell this from dirt and stones?" Eogan sounded intrigued. "Isn't something more definite needed?"

"You mean like the body of a dead alien?"

"It might help prove your theory."

"I don't need your sarcasm." She crossed her arms.

"I did not intend to disrespect you." He tone was apologetic.

Hester felt her ire dissipate. It was difficult to be angry with a man who was so gorgeous and had just saved her life.

"It's only an idea. That's why I want to see the site for myself. I might get some insight into what the inscriptions mean, or what the complex was intended for."

Eogan leaned over the steering wheel as he maneuvered the jeep into a small enclosure. It was a tented structure, and once inside, he shut the engine off. He opened the door and stepped out. Someone would have to be walking nearby to see the jeep.

"You'll get a chance to inspect your stones now. We have to leave the vehicle in case it's found. It might have a tracking device on it."

She grabbed her backpack and pulled out a flashlight. "Great."

Eogan reached into the rear seat and started to rummage around until he hauled out a first aid kit. He slammed the door closed and waited for Hester to join him before exiting the shelter and pulling the netted material down over the entrance. The jeep was completely concealed.

"Where do we go?"

Hester swung her light. "The ruins of course."

Eogan held her arm and helped her down the side of a gravelly hill. "We must stay hidden. You can examine them as long as it's safe."

A jolt of heat raced through Hester's body.

She wasn't certain if it was Eogan's touch or the thought of seeing the monoliths up close. It was silly to think that he would ever mean anything to her. After all, he'd as much as admitted that he wasn't interested in women. Besides, gorgeous men didn't notice her. She'd accepted that long ago and had pushed any romantic thoughts out of her head forever.

"How much further?" Eogan had stopped to scan the area. "I need to remove something."

"Take it off here."

"It is not sheltered enough."

"There might be someplace in the ruins. The main area is under cover now and they usually have tents set up for excavation finds."

Hester pointed her light to an indentation in the ground. The top of a steel roof was reflected in her beam. Below the structure, T-shaped pillars were visible. Her stomach tightened and she had to force herself to breathe. After years of research, she was close to finding out if her theory was true. To see the stones that might be a link to an ancient alien culture was more than she had ever hoped.

Her life was routine and comfortable. Her days filled with teaching and helping at insignificant digs in the summer months. She did most of her alternative history research in the evenings and on weekends. This didn't stop her from craving adventure, though. Never in her wildest dreams had she thought she might explore one of the sites that she'd studied.

They climbed down a steep incline, and entered an area of steel poles and metal roofing.

Hester inhaled a sharp breath when she saw the first stone.

She let her light rest on the grooves and holes carved into the tall pillar. She ran a shaky hand up the rock as far as she could reach, letting her fingers feel it's indentations as if she were reading braille. It sent a thrill from her fingers to the tips of her toes. She didn't want to miss anything. When she'd felt all sides, she stepped back and let her flashlight beam linger on the figure of a lizard-like animal carved in a downward direction. It was poised as if ready to pounce.

She moved her light to the adjacent stone and then the next, until she'd highlighted every pillar in the circle. She reached into her backpack and pulled out a camera.

"Can you hold the light on this?" Hester handed Eogan the flashlight.

He grunted, but he held the beam steady. She clicked a couple of shots and then moved to another stone. The carvings were spectacular. The pictures would go a long way in helping with her research. She swallowed back her excitement. She had to stay focused.

"There's another structure to the east. Can we go there?"

Eogan helped her up the side of the mound and followed her the short distance to the nearby circle.

She photographed each stone and was ready to move on when the sound of a distant rumbling broke through the air. She looked up at him for direction, but he was staring at the structure with a frown.

"What?" she asked.

He shook his head. "This is familiar."

"You've probably seen it in textbooks, or on the web."

"I don't have access to those."

"That's impossible." Hester scoffed. "Everyone has the internet."

"I am kept in a cell." His voice was cold. "I am not given such privileges."

"Have you escaped from prison?"

Hester's voice quivered as she recalled how easily he had dispatched those men. What if she was talking with a serial killer and he meant for her to be his next victim. She gave herself a mental shake. If he were a murderer, he would have hardly let her come to this place and take pictures.

"Not in the sense that you mean." Eogan took a step back. "I do remember seeing something like this when I was a child."

"You grew up in Turkey?" Hester climbed up beside him. "Did your parents bring you here for a visit?"

"I have no parents."

"Were you an orphan?"

"No."

"That doesn't make sense." Hester walked to another section. "Does that mean you were raised by foster parents?"

"I was trained by teachers until I was ten and then..." Eogan's voice faded.

Hester turned. "You remembered."

"Yes." He pointed at the largest circle. "They resemble a vibration system for creating energy."

Chapter 5

"Where is it from?" Hester's voice was filled with excitement.

"It's an ancient system. I've only seen remnants in the records of other planets."

She stopped so quickly that Eogan almost ran into her.

"You know about other worlds?"

He hesitated a second. To admit he wasn't from Earth was risky. Still, Hester was an unusual person. He had seldom been near women, but they had never wanted to explore old rocks and sand mounds. She'd almost died at the hands of a group of mercenaries and she'd shaken it off the moment she came to this place.

Time was essential to removing the device in his neck, and yet he couldn't bring himself to stop Hester from exploring these standing stone circles. It was more than obeying a woman. He had a strange compulsion to do what she wished. She was happy and as long as they weren't in any immediate danger, they could stay.

"The records say they aren't in use anymore." Eogan decided to ease into the truth. She didn't need to know where he'd learned about them. "They were utilized in the initial terraforming of some planets. The mechanisms were meant to last eons, and the odd one that remains standing, still works."

"So this is producing energy." Hester's voice was soft with awe. "I wonder if it's something that can be measured."

"I am not knowledgeable about these things. The ones in the records were not made of granite."

He wanted to keep moving. He took Hester's arm and led her to the next pillar, which was T-shaped. It was one of the largest and stood in the middle of the ring. It was mounted on bedrock. Across from it was another stone. Both monoliths were over sixteen feet tall and even though they looked identical, when his hands roamed over the surface, he could feel that they had unique engravings.

They were the same and yet different from the ones he'd seen in the records. Those had been made of metal posts, with gold connecting rods between them.

"How do they work?"

"Power could be directed downward and concentrated on the center of the structure, which conducted energy to the other components around the circle and set up a perpetual wave vibration."

"It seems complicated." She ran her fingers across the column. "I wonder if these were ever started."

"They look like replicas." Eogan watched as Hester focused the lens of her camera. "You would need metal to conduct energy."

"You don't think they were ever activated." Hester took a picture of the megalith. "How long would an apparatus like that vibrate for?"

"The old systems that were intact and standing, still had residual vibrations. The structures deteriorate over time. Age and neglect are the enemy of these mechanisms."

"Maybe that's why there are so many UFO sightings and supposed aliens on Earth." She walked to the opposite stone. "They're trying to repair or build a new system?"

"The ancients who built these structures have long since left this galaxy."

Hester sighed. "What a shame. It would be great to meet an alien."

"Only if they were non-threatening."

Eogan's voice was dry. She was an extraordinary person and very accepting. Most humans would have screamed denials if he'd told them that he'd seen these structures in other planets' records. Instead, Hester had calmly asked what their purpose was. For a human, she was a rarity.

Hester swung around and pointed her flashlight at his chest. "I just realized you said that you'd seen them in other planet archives. Are these accounts in the hands of another group of Ufologist?"

"I don't know of such an organization."

Hester's eyes narrowed. "You must belong to one of them. You don't have access to the internet and that's the only other place you could get this information."

"I saw them on other planets." He held his breath as he waited for her reaction. Truth between them was imperative. She needed to understand her life was at risk by staying with him.

The stillness of the night became magnified. The only interruption was the soft swishing of bats flying overhead and the scurrying of small lizards on the gravel. Hester halted and stood as if a statue, and for a few seconds, Eogan wondered if she'd stopped breathing. There was a gasp and then she laughed.

It was a quiet chuckle.

"I thought you said you'd been to other planets." She walked to the ramp. "I must have been more rattled by those men than I thought. Unless there is a new space program I've never heard about, no one has visited other worlds. Great story about the circles being used for energy, though."

So she'd misinterpreted his words. It was best. The fewer humans who knew about the existence of Hunters the better. He looked human, so she'd accepted him as being human.

"We need to leave."

"I haven't heard any vehicles. You lost the car that was following us ages ago." Hester climbed the incline and went toward another megalith. "Why do you think you're being chased?"

"They ambushed the group I was deployed with." Eogan reached for her arm. "It is not safe to remain in this place."

"I traveled for three days to get here. Men have died. I'm not leaving right away."

She was stubborn.

He admired that.

A strong woman was an honor to serve. They knew what they wanted and it was easier to follow their commands. If she desired to be here in this replica of an ancient energy machine, then he would oblige her for a few more minutes. He took a step back and scanned the horizon. At the moment there was no sign of vehicles or pursuit. That could be deceptive.

He knew the military and the Albireons had weapons at their disposal that most people had no knowledge of. The earth's populace was not aware of everything that occurred on this planet. Only a few humans knew the extent of the alien technology exchanges or clandestine activities and experiments that were sanctioned.

Eogan followed Hester to the next circle and waited a few steps behind as she got down on her knees to explore the plinth of another pillar. A structure made of metal would still be emitting a residual energy which would affect the planet. If there had been a working mechanism here, the Albireons would have guarded it.

"Could you take this?" Hester held out her flashlight. "I want to try and get a picture of this engraving. It reminds me of a carving I saw on one of my digs."

"Are they connected?" Eogan aimed the flashlight so it shone on the monolith.

"It's not the same, but there are some familiar strokes." She crouched down close and focused the camera lens. "If I can get a picture I'll be able to compare it later."

"One more photo and then I must insist we stop. It is imperative I remove my implant."

There was a soft clicking accompanied by flashes of light. Hester didn't seem to be listening to him. She was intent on her task until she'd stopped shooting. She looked at him as she stood up.

"What do you mean by implants?" She glanced down at her camera viewing screen. "Are you referring to Radio Frequency Identification chips? I thought they only put them in clothing or credit cards."

"Those are primitive locators."

"A lot of people think you can be followed with those things." Hester groaned. "These pictures aren't great, but I'm not going to get anything better in this light. Maybe we could stay here until sunrise."

Her voice ended on a hopeful tone. Eogan's chest tightened. He hated to deny her, but time was important. They had wasted precious minutes exploring the archaeological site. After his implant was removed, he needed to contact the other Hunters and get Hester to safety.

"We have to leave." Eogan tried to soften the tone of his refusal. "It's risky for you to be with me."

Hester frowned. "Maybe I should stay here and let you continue on your own. I've delayed you long enough, especially if people are chasing you."

"I can't abandoned you here."

Honor demanded he protect her until she was safe. Being with him had endangered her life. If the general's men knew she had even seen him, she would be at risk. It had been crazy to take her with him, but there had been no other options. When she'd pleaded to stay with him, he couldn't deny her.

"I've come this far on my own."

He touched her arm and almost jumped back as a shock raced up his fingers. He had contact with numerous humans in the past thirty years and none of them had affected him in this manner. Perhaps there was a residual power flowing from these ruins after all. They needed to leave this area.

"The men pursuing me will kill you if they find us together," he said.

Hester put her camera in her backpack. "You sound paranoid."

"It is my reality." Eogan's tone was serious. He realized it was hard for her to believe him, yet he had to make her appreciate how precarious her situation was. Her chances of being harmed increased the longer she stayed with him.

"What kind of place did you escape from?" There was doubt in her voice.

"I am a military weapon." Eogan stated the truth. "The people who control me, do not work within your rules."

"Do you mean the laws of Turkey?"

"Earth." His voice was low. "These men do not answer to other humans."

There was a few seconds of silence. "When you said you'd seen records from other planets did these people show them to you?"

"I saw them before I crashed here." Eogan kept his voice calm.

"Are you saying that you're from another planet?"

"Yes." Eogan needed her to understand the danger she was in by being with him. "We have to keep moving before I'm caught."

"So you weren't joking earlier."

Eogan shook his head. "It is important for me to remove the implant in my neck."

Hester exhaled a deep breath. "Promise I'll be able to come back here one day."

"Once you are safe, you can go anywhere you want." Eogan took her hand. He ignored the shock of awareness that coursed through him and led her away from the circle of pillars. "You must never let anyone know you were with me. That knowledge would put your life in danger. Next time, I might not be able to save you."

"Great." Hester ran beside him. "I finally get to meet an alien and I can't talk about it."

"Aren't you concerned about what I told you?"

"I've been dreaming of proving that UFO's are real for years." Hester's breathing was ragged. "I've studied everything I could find and it all leads to a brick wall. It's as if the government doesn't want us to know."

"They don't." Eogan slowed so that Hester could catch her breath.

"They are using the data that they get from other aliens to try and improve their own technology. It is not something they want to make public to the whole populace."

"Why not?" Hester's voice held frustration. "We're not stupid. We have a right to know what is happening on our planet."

Eogan couldn't argue with her. He agreed. Unfortunately, there were too many interested groups involved in covering up the real extent of the corruption and secrecy on this planet. He'd heard of such things on other worlds during his training, but he had never expected to spend thirty years of his life subjugated to concealed supremacies.

"Those who are in power do not want others to interfere with their plans."

"Secrets are never good." Hester stopped and bent over to catch her breath. "How can you run so fast?"

"It is easy on this planet." Eogan tried to control his impatience. In the distance he thought he caught the sound of a vehicle. "You are out of shape."

"True." Hester stood. "I spend all my time slouched over a computer or in the library doing research. Moving books is the most cardio activity I get."

"We need to go. Can you run?"

"I'll be fine." Hester took off ahead, the light from her flashlight showing the way. In the distance, Eogan saw the outline of a tented structure. He pointed toward it and redirected Hester. They ran for a few more minutes in silence until they reached the shelter.

It was tiny and leaned against a dirt mound.

"This will do." Eogan pulled the flap open and let Hester enter first. "The hill should keep our light out of view."

"Whatever you think is best." Hester flopped down on the ground. "I need a break. My lungs can't stand anymore."

"What do your lungs have to do with hiding?"

"Nothing." Hester dug out a bit of earth and put her flashlight in it. The beam shone up onto the tarp roof of their hiding spot. "They make it easier to breathe though. I'd hate to collapse on you."

"I would carry you."

"Nice to know."

Hester's mouth tilted into a grin and Eogan's stomach did a flip at the sight. He frowned. Never in his life, not even on the most treacherous missions, had his body ever reacted like this. He hoped he hadn't been poisoned. He'd been careful not to take any food that had been offered to him on his journey out to this country. Still, they might have found a way to inject him without his knowing. The other option was his implant was controlling him in a way he wasn't aware of.

The sooner he got rid of the device, and got Hester to safety, the better. He plopped the first aid kit he'd brought from the car down on the ground. He flipped it open and rummaged through its contents. It was a basic set, but it had what he needed. He pulled out a pair of scissors and a blade.

"What do you need those for?"

"It is necessary to dig out the implant." Eogan shrugged off his jacket. "I may need your help."

He heard the whirr of an engine.

It was near.

"Turn off the flashlight."

Hester shut off the light. "Are they close?"

"They have reached the site. If they find the vehicle we hid, then they'll know we're here."

Brakes screeched to a stop and the slam of a car door echoed through the still night air. In minutes they would be found. Hiding wasn't the answer. The only other option was to run and they were too far away from the jeep to do that.

He had to take the offensive and surprise them.

He pulled his gun out of his waistband, released the cartridge and checked the bullets. He inhaled and eased his breathing.

"I won't be long."

Chapter 6

"You can't leave me here alone." Hester's heart started pounding at a frantic pace. "Let me come with you."

"No." He handed her the flashlight. "I don't know how many men there are. It will be best if you stay here."

The horror of what had happened at the roadside came flooding back. She remembered the ease with which Eogan had destroyed her attackers. There was no hesitation or emotion behind his actions. He'd called himself a military weapon, and he was right. He'd walked into a group of armed men and decimated them within seconds.

"You're going to kill them."

Eogan's silence was confirmation enough.

Somehow, she wasn't surprised by that fact. It made sense in a macabre sort of way. It was survival at its most basic level. These men wouldn't stop following them and if the ones that had shot her friends were any indication, death was the only solution. They were a ruthless lot and strangely enough, she didn't feel any horror at the fact that they might lose their lives. It was as if she were distanced from the whole situation.

She gave herself a mental shake.

It must be the aftereffects of shock.

When had she gone from a peace-loving archaeology professor to someone who could understand the need to take a life? It was true that they were ruthless men, who taunted and then murdered her companions without hesitation. They had been cruel and brutal, and the logical part of her knew that before they had attacked her, they'd left many victims in their wake.

That didn't excuse her condoning murder.

Self-defense was another thing, though.

"Promise you'll only execute them if they're the ones following you."

"There would be no honor in harming an innocent man." He frowned.

Hester wasn't reassured. "I'm going with you. I have to be certain that these people are part of the same group before you harm them."

"A warrior doesn't lie. It is safer for you to stay here." Eogan's voice was insistent. "There is only one vehicle, so I will have no problem."

"It's my fault they found you." Hester lifted her chin. "I should have listened and left when you wanted to go."

"They would have located me anyway." His tone softened. "I have endangered your life. I will take care of this threat, and then we'll remove the device in my neck."

Hester bit her lip. "What if you need help?"

"I would worry about your safety if you accompanied me." He opened the tent flap. "Stay here until I come back."

Eogan left and Hester shivered in the silence. It was just her luck that she'd finally met an alien and he was determined to kill people. Still, he'd saved her life and for that, she'd be forever grateful. She'd have to trust him.

If Eogan was truly an extraterrestrial, he was different than she'd envisioned. He didn't look anything like the pictures she saw on the internet. They were all bizarre beings with either grey or scaly skin. They had large eyes and no mouths. There had been one site that showed human-like creatures with blonde hair though. Maybe Eogan came from their homeland.

He appeared to be human.

That presented a problem.

Logic and reason dictated that he was as human as she was, and that meant he wasn't from another planet. What a fool she was. She wanted to meet someone from outer space so desperately that she was willing to accept whatever she was told. She was a trained archaeologist. She knew that the scientific method should be applied whenever she was looking at something new. She'd thrown all of her training out the window the minute she'd started looking at these ancient sites. She'd allowed herself to be hoodwinked into believing the most outlandish story.

Of course Eogan was from Earth.

He was probably an escapee from a mental hospital.

Hester's fingers gripped her flashlight tighter. If that were the case, then she was in danger. She couldn't remain with him. So far the only people he'd been violent with had deserved it, but what if he turned on her? Dare she risk going out in the night by herself? She tried to remember where they'd parked the jeep. All she had to do was find it and then she could take off back to town.

At least she thought she could.

She hadn't been paying attention to the direction they'd been traveling in when they left Sanliurfa. She'd blindly trusted the men she'd accepted a ride with and let them take control of the excursion. Why had she allowed herself to be talked into going with Steve and Franklin in the first place? The only contact she'd ever had with them had been on the internet.

She'd met Steve on an alternative history chatroom, and when he'd introduced her to Franklin, they'd seemed like great companions. They'd been to Gobekli Tepe many times and they'd assured her there were no risks. Her initial plan had been to scope the city out and book a daytime tour of the site. A lot of tourists visited the ruins, so it had seemed safe.

She'd left a quick note for her mother and father, and then took off. Her parents considered the Middle East too dangerous for a woman alone, and had used all their influence in the past to convince her to stay away. Hindsight proved them right. She'd almost died, and now she was partnered with a lunatic.

At least life wasn't boring.

She was on an honest to goodness adventure.

She had to risk leaving on her own, and getting to the city. Who knew what would happen to her if she stayed with Eogan? He seemed a nice guy, but psychopaths were manipulative. Men never paid attention to her, so she knew he didn't have any ulterior motives for keeping her with him. Besides, she was the one who had begged him to let her come.

Still, she hesitated.

Why was she so reluctant to leave?

She was comfortable with Eogan. There was a sense of security and acceptance with him. He hadn't made fun of her desire to see the ruins. He'd even held the flashlight and let her take pictures despite his urgency to get some microchip removed from his body. Having an implant sounded like the stories told by humans who claimed they'd been abducted by beings from outer space.

There was always the possibility he was an alien shapeshifter.

Now she was letting her imagination run wild. It was ludicrous, and her logical brain said they didn't exist. Still, she believed that extraterrestrials were visiting Earth, so why couldn't they have unusual abilities. The possibilities were endless.

The only thing she could trust, was that she was human and needed to get to safety. Hester straightened her shoulders. She lifted the flap of the tent, but before she could leave, Eogan stumbled inside.

He threw some guns on the floor beside her.

She'd never seen so many rifles before. There was a hand grenade or two in the cache also. She glanced up at him. He was as calm as if he'd been out shopping.

"Are these real?" Hester's voice shook.

"Pretend weapons wouldn't help us."

"Did you hurt them?"

"They are dead." He sat on the ground and reached for the flashlight. He buried it in the dirt. "There were six of them. I didn't hesitate once I realized that they were looking for me."

"Oh." Her eyes widened. "Doesn't it bother you to kill people?"

"Death is never easy." He grabbed the first aid supplies. "It's what I've been trained to do since I was ten years old."

"That's awfully young to start fighting." Hester kept her voice steady. The tiny voice of self-preservation inside her head was telling her to humor him. "Were you a child soldier?"

"What is that?"

"Children in areas of conflict are often forced to join armies."

"I fight because that's what I've been created to do. I am clan Rioge, and bred to command."

"That must have been a difficult childhood." Hester's voice drifted away as she watched him. He rolled the sleeve up on his left arm, removed a strip of material, and held his arm out to her. There was a cut about an inch long on his forearm and fresh blood on his skin.

"This is where the other implant was."

"You did that to yourself?" Disbelief and horror filled Hester. She couldn't imagine deliberately slicing her arm open.

"There was no other way."

"How long ago?"

"Before I met you." He rummaged in the first aid kit. "This is the first chance I've had to attend to it."

Hester shuddered and forced back nausea when she saw the blood that was still oozing from his wound. He acted as if there were no pain. He wiped the cut with a clean gauze and then used a couple of steri-strips to close the incision.

"Will that hold?"

"I heal quickly." He passed her a blade from the first aid kit. "I am going to need your help for the last device."

"You can't expect me to cut you open!"

Hester didn't hide her disbelief. Eogan had told her about the device he needed removed, but it hadn't seemed real. She'd read about these things being in people who claimed that they'd been abducted by aliens. She didn't really believe it though. It seemed a lot of trouble just to keep track of someone. If a superior being was watching humans, wouldn't they have something more sophisticated to locate people?

"It does more than find people. That one was for enhancements and modifications. The chips in my clothing were for tracking."

For a brief second Hester had the uncanny sensation that Eogan had read her thoughts.

That was impossible.

He pulled out an alcohol swab and cleaned the blade. "The next one is more complicated. It is attached to my spinal cord."

He felt behind his neck and she watched his fingers trace his cervical vertebrae.

"I can't do that." Hester shook her head. "The sight of blood makes me sick."

"You must." His tone was serious. "If you want I will do the initial cut, but you have to detach it and pull it out."

"Are you kidding?" Hester swallowed her hysteria. "A surgeon should do something like that. This place isn't sterile."

He held the blade out to her. "There is no other choice."

"There are always options." She leaned away from him.

"If you don't remove it, I will die."

Chapter 7

A myriad of emotions passed over Hester's face.

The light in the tent was too dim for him to see her face clearly. Somehow, he was sensing her reactions. Her fingers shook. He clasped them in his hand and held them steady. He had to convince her to conquer her fear and aid him. If he removed the implant himself, there was no guarantee that he'd be successful. His best course of action was to have Hester help him.

"You won't hurt me."

"You can't ask someone to dig something out of your body." Her voice trembled. "What if I do something wrong and you die?"

"I have been in their control for too many years." Eogan kept his voice calm. "Death would be welcomed."

"It could be worse." Hester's fingers fluttered in his hand. "I could hit a nerve and you'd be paralyzed. If my hands shake and I damage something, you might be in agony for the rest of your life."

"Pain is a part of life for a Hunter."

Hester gave him a sharp glance. "A hunter as in killing animals?"

"A Hunter that is a warrior."

"Like those urban legends on the internet?"

"I haven't heard these myths."

"A group called aHunter4Hire supposedly goes around saving people and exacting justice." She leaned closer to him. "You can only contact them through the internet and it's very secretive. I think it's a bunch of lies. It's probably a government scheme to gather personal information on us. Are you pretending to be one of them?"

"My breed is called Hunters. We are an ancient warrior race created and modified to be the best soldiers in the universe."

"So it's a coincidence that you have the same name as an internet hoax?"

There was doubt in Hester's voice. Her skepticism had replaced her fear. He wasn't certain if his brother Hunters had started this group or not, but Hester was distracted enough to forget her qualms about helping him.

"I don't know." Eogan released her fingers and picked up the razor blade. "If you direct my arm, I will hold the light so you can see."

"This is insane." Hester's voice was a low whisper. "I wanted adventure, but nothing like this. I should have remembered what my mother used to say about being careful about what you wish for."

"Your mother sounds like a wise woman." Eogan placed the blade in her hand. "I can see where you get your strength from."

"I'm weak." Hester took the blade and twisted it in her fingers so that the cutting edge was outward. "I'm afraid of my own shadow. That's why I decided to come here without telling anyone. I didn't want to hear about all the things I should be frightened of."

"You are sensible as well as strong." He turned his back to her. "That is rare on this planet because women are not allowed to rule."

"I suppose they are in control where you come from?" Hester's tone was sarcastic.

"Women command and men obey."

"That's a switch." Hester exhaled a heavy breath. "You need to show me where to cut."

Eogan lifted the flashlight. "Guide my arm so that the light shines on my neck.

A jolt of sensation went through him when Hester touched him.

The sooner the implant came out, the better. There was no reason for his handlers to influence his body now, especially if they thought he was dead. It had been done all too often in the past. Perhaps they were testing to see if he was still alive. The Albireons had been relentless in their experiments with injections and brain impulses until they had him under their complete authority.

It had taken months of focus and discipline to free himself from a small amount of their manipulation. As soon as they realized they'd lost influence, the Albireons would alter the charges they were sending to his body. Eogan had become adept at pretending he was in their power. Once he'd met Partlan and knew that there were other Hunters alive on this planet, he'd concentrated all of his energy on overcoming the last of the controls that General Carter and the Albireons had over him in preparation for his escape.

He thought he'd succeeded.

It was obvious they had more sway than he realized.

With his other hand he felt for the bulge at the base of his skull. This was where she needed to cut if he was ever going to be free of the

Albireons. It was a slight indentation beside his upper cervical vertebra.

"Can you see it?"

Hester leaned against his back. He felt her breath against his skin and a tingle of awareness raced over him. It was a novel sensation being so close to another being. He had been in confinement for the past six months, but even before that, he was isolated from other humans unless he was on assignment.

"It's not very big." Hester's voice was hesitant. "Are you sure you want me to do this?"

"It is necessary."

"What if it bleeds?"

"Wipe it away." Eogan kept his voice steady. "It will stop and then you can continue."

"Okay." Hester's finger brushed his neck and then she swabbed it with alcohol. "This will hurt."

"Do what you must."

His muscles tensed as the sting of the blade sliced his skin.

Hester inhaled. "There's blood, but I can see a tiny metal thing."

"It's attached. Pick at it until you can see the ends," Eogan explained in a firm voice. "You will need to tease the strands away before you can remove it."

"It sounds easy enough."

Hester was silent for a few seconds. Eogan felt a slight pull on his skin and then another slice of the blade. The implant must be deeper than he had thought. That was due to the length of time it had been in his body. Hester leaned closer to him.

"Hold the light a bit higher."

Eogan adjusted his arm.

There was a sharp shock of pain down one side of his body. It was followed by another jolt down the opposite side. Adrenaline rushed through him seconds before his body started to shake. Eogan lost consciousness. He came to with a feeling of elation. Everything was brighter. It was as if he'd been wearing sunglasses his whole life. His hearing and sense of smell were hypersensitive and for the first time in thirty years he was free.

Free from control.

Free to be a Hunter.

He needed to contact the other Hunters that Partlan had told him about. They would be able to help in his escape. That was the only way that he would be truly free from the Albireons and the humans they were allied with.

"Are you okay?" Hester shook his shoulder. "I thought I'd killed you."

"It is difficult to destroy a Hunter." He was proud of being a Hunter for the first time in over thirty years. He was no longer a puppet forced to do the bidding of others. He did not have to work for people with abhorrent motives.

"That's easy for you to say. You were unconscious." She held a metal object in front of him. "Here is the implant."

Eogan sat upright and reached for it. "This is an old model."

"It might be old to you, but I've never seen anything like it." Hester leaned close and pointed at the strands that stuck out at each side. "These were buried within your muscles."

"It was to be expected." He put the device on the ground and slammed it with a rock. It shattered into pieces. "It was inserted when I was twenty."

"You're not old enough for it to have worked its way into you that deep."

"I have seen over forty years."

She sat back on her feet. "That's impossible. You don't look older than twenty-five."

"This planet is good for me."

"I'll say." Hester reached for a steri-strip. "It's a big incision so I have to close it. That's the only way it'll stop bleeding."

He turned so she could reach him. "You are a very brave women. I thank you for saving my life."

"You're not out of the woods yet."

Her fingers touch his neck. Another jolt of sensation rushed through him. Every nerve of his body was aware of her. His heart started to beat at a rapid pace when she leaned closer. This made no sense. The implant was removed and he was still feeling this strange reaction to Hester. It had never happened in all the years that he'd been on this planet.

She put another strip on and a tremor ran through him.

"There." Hester moved away. "You're all patched up. Now, I want some answers."

Eogan rubbed the back of his neck. The wound was about an inch long. "I told you everything."

"You barely scratched the surface of what I want to know." Hester pointed to the ruined implant on the ground. "Where did that device come from?"

"It was inserted while I was in captivity."

Hester nodded. "You tried to tell me before, but I didn't believe it."

"A Hunter does not lie."

"I understand that now, but could we please go over the details once more. Why are you here and who is chasing you? This time, I promise to pay close attention."

Eogan blinked at the transformed woman who sat in front of him. There was no fear or uncertainty in her voice. Her arms were crossed and an eyebrow was raised. It was as if he were seeing her for the first time. She was small compared to him, yet her thick, dark-framed glasses and posture gave her an aura of command. His respect and appreciation for Hester grew. She deserved the whole truth about him.

"I was sent to Earth on a mission when I was fifteen years old." Eogan watched Hester's face in the dim beam of the flashlight. "It was a training assignment and our teachers were present. I was the only one of Rioge clan. The rest of the Hunters were Saidir clan."

"You have clans like the Celts?"

"I do not know these Celts. We are birthed into clans. Rioge clan is bred to lead."

"Isn't that earned?" Hester's voice showed doubt.

"We are genetically modified to be the best warriors. Each clan has a specialty. Giath clan are fantastic shooters, Obair clan are experts in firearms and machines, and Leigh clan are healers. I am Rioge clan. We lead."

She nodded. "What planet are you from?|

"Cygnus."

"What was your mission on Earth?"

"I was not told. After we crashed, I was ordered to stay at the collision site so that the military would find me. The other survivors escaped."

"Were you going to act as a spy?" She leaned forward, her voice full of excitement. "Infiltrate and then report back to your teachers."

"I was bait. It was expected that the humans would take me away and forget about the others. Even under torture I would never disclose the location of my fellow warriors."

"Oh." Hester inhaled a sharp breath. "That wasn't fair."

Eogan started to pack up the first aid kit. "It's an honor to sacrifice ourselves so that our brothers can live to fight another day."

"What if you don't want to?"

"I have been bred to follow orders." He handed the medical gear to Hester. "There is no other option."

"That doesn't sound like much of a life." She put the kit into her backpack.

"A Hunter lives to obey and die with honor."

"Now you're scaring me." She clutched her bag to her chest. "At first I thought you were just a bit paranoid or had escaped from a mental hospital."

"The people chasing me are real."

"And they have held you captive?"

"For over thirty years." Eogan handed Hester the flashlight. "They have used me as a weapon. They have tracked me and controlled my actions so that I have had no other choice but to do their wishes."

"So this is genuine." A tremor ran through her. "I've always wanted to meet an alien, but you don't look like anything I imagined. You look human."

"Most of my genes are identical to yours." Eogan reached over and switched the flashlight off. "It is important to leave this area. I will try to find my brothers and get help."

"There are others like you on Earth."

"Many of us." Eogan pushed through the tent opening. "There are the survivors from when I crashed and since then, there have been new Hunters who are also stranded on this planet."

"Why didn't they rescue you?" Hester followed him out of the enclosure.

"They didn't know I was alive." Eogan walked over a wooden ramp. "My ability to communicate with them was blocked."

"That makes sense." Hester ran to keep up with him. "What about where you were locked up? There must have been some people who would have helped you escape."

"The humans there were under the control of the Albireons."

"What are Albireons?"

"They are beings from another galaxy who have been on this planet for over seventy years."

"I knew it." Hester's voice rose in excitement. "The people I talk with say that there are many different aliens already on Earth. How many species are here?"

"I only know about the Albireons."

"We should be able to communicate with them. Think of the information they could share with us."

"The Albireons are not your friends. They want to destroy humans."

Chapter 8

Hester's heart skipped a beat at the seriousness of Eogan's last words. All of her research pointed to the existence of aliens, and it had always been a possibility that any beings visiting Earth would be hostile. It didn't seem likely that these Albireons would have stayed here for seventy years and not attacked.

Then again, Eogan had just admitted that he was from another planet, and he'd saved her life. Was he likely to lie to her about something so serious?

"You've been locked away so how do you know this?"

"This is not the first time Albireons have threatened a world. They have succeeded numerous times." Eogan's voice was harsh. "They have already taken command of most of Earth's resources."

"That's no different than what various multinational corporations have done."

"They hold humans hostage and experiment on them to harvest their DNA." His tone was scornful. "Are these the aliens you're so anxious to meet?"

Hester's research had come across numerous abduction stories. The victims had all suffered pain, torture, and memory loss. She'd considered each case individually and still didn't know how many were real. There was no doubt in Eogan's voice. If what he said was true, then there was a severe threat to humanity that was being kept secret.

"Why would our politicians hide something this serious?"

"I don't know if your governments know of the existence of the Albireons. Many influential people have allied with them. They are not in the direct administration of any countries."

"Why would these people do that?"

"They think that the Albireons will give them power." Eogan kept walking toward the jeep.

"It's about making a profit." Hester didn't bother to hide her contempt. She might be an untenured archaeology professor, but she knew how the world worked. Those with the financial clout were the ones in control.

"It is possible. On Cygnus there was no need for money."

"It's an exchange of information. That is where the real power is." Hester shifted her backpack. "They're making a fortune on new technology."

"They believe that the Albireons will protect them when the planet is destroyed. They are wrong."

Hester's breath caught in her throat. "What do you mean by destroyed?"

"Albireons are the scourge of the universe. They have been driven out of most planetary systems where the inhabitants have the ability to travel in space."

"Why?"

"Their real purpose is to make money and they do that by gene collection and manipulation. They create designer species and store the genes of species that they have forced into extinction."

"So they end up with a monopoly on the genetic code of those they have annihilated?" Hester was trying to understand what Eogan was telling her. It sounded like something from a science fiction novel and even though she had training in biology, none of that dealt with genetic manipulation.

"They collect and then profit because the genes are rare." Eogan clasped her arm.

A tingle of sensation raced through her body. Her breath caught in her throat and her heart beat faster. There was no doubt about her reaction. She was standing in the middle of Gobekli Tepe with an honest to goodness alien, and she was attracted to him.

He was gorgeous, but she knew better than to expect him to notice her. Men always looked past her, whether it was at a club, a dance, or in the classroom. She had given up her fairy tale dreams of meeting her Prince Charming in her teens. Instead, she'd buried herself in her studies. It was easier and less painful to avoid men. They never noticed her, so it took no effort to do. Now, for the first time in her life, she found herself attracted to a man.

Not just any man.

He was an alien.

"The collection of genetic material is not why they are held in contempt by most evolved planets." Eogan continued to speak as he helped her down the hill. "It is how they collect their material that makes them contemptible."

"They capture people and steal their genes." She forced her voice to remain steady. "Isn't that despicable enough?"

"That is part of it." He released her and pointed in the direction of another mound. "The vehicle is there."

Hester gave herself a mental shake. She'd become totally turned around in the dark. There was no way she would have been able to locate the jeep on her own. She'd made the right decision staying with Eogan. Now she needed to know more about this alien threat he was speaking about.

"What is the other part?"

"The Albireons destroy the planets that they steal genetic codes from."

It took Hester a couple of seconds to assimilate the full implication of what Eogan had said. She took a deep breath and stopped walking. She must have heard wrong, because what he was suggesting wasn't possible. He continued to move toward the jeep. When he noticed she wasn't following, he waited.

"Are you saying that they will destroy Earth when they are finished with us?"

"Yes." He motioned her forward. "We need to leave."

"I'm still stuck on the part about my planet being destroyed." Hester refused to move.

He walked back to her. "There is nothing we can do standing here. I have information that might help my fellow warriors try to defeat the Albireons. If we are caught, they will not get the material."

"Fair enough." She nodded and followed him to the jeep. "I'm coming with you. If there are aliens on this planet that plan to destroy the human race then I need to know about it. The rest of the world should be told."

"No one will believe you." Eogan started the vehicle and backed it out of the hiding place. "You did not accept that I wasn't from Earth."

"That's because you look human. Other than a strange need to kill people, you seem pretty normal to me."

"I only execute others when it is necessary or when I am following orders."

"We could argue that all night. Right now, I need to know about these Albireons." Hester wasn't going to let him keep her from knowing the truth. "Where are they?"

"They live underground." Eogan pulled onto the road. "Usually below military bases."

"So the government must know about their plans."

He sped up as soon as they were away from Gobekli Tepe. "Your governments have made treaties with the Albireons in the hopes that they will not attack Earth."

"That makes sense."

She couldn't fault their logic. They were working with an alien race that was obviously further advanced than humans. They could be risking total destruction if they didn't agree to a treaty. There was only one problem that Hester saw.

"If they work below military bases, how come the government hasn't figured out what their real agenda is?"

"The Albireons have too much power now." Eogan drove toward the lights of Sanliurfa in the distance. "It would require the combined efforts of all countries on this planet in order to defeat them."

"And none of the world powers are willing to do that." Hester finished in a dry tone. "They all want the technology so that they can create better weapons."

"They have those ordnances already." He looked at her. "Now, it is a problem of maintaining the status quo. No one wants to admit that they are afraid. It is a matter of national pride."

"They're playing chicken with the human race." Hester swallowed back her disgust.

"What does a bird have to do with the Albireons' plan to destroy Earth?" Eogan's tone was hesitant.

"It's a saying to describe two people charging at each other at full tilt, and each hoping the other one swerves away first. Neither side is willing to admit that they might be wrong because it would look weak."

"That is a strange term for what they are doing. You are right, though." Eogan eased his speed as they approached the outer edge of the city. "It would be better to help each other."

"It's obvious you were kept locked away from the reality of what happens on this planet." Hester looked out the window. She couldn't believe that a man as intelligent as Eogan didn't have a clue about what motivated humans.

"I understand your species better than you think."

She gave him a sharp look. "Can you hear my thoughts?"

"That is not possible with humans."

Hester leaned back. It had to be a coincidence that he had spoken about what she had just been considering. People didn't read minds. There were some who claimed to be clairvoyant and psychic, but that wasn't the same. Just in case, she'd better have a care about what she was thinking.

"Where are we going?"

"I am going to continue my mission." Eogan pulled over to the side of the road. "I will take you home. Where is your hotel?"

"You're planning to dump me?"

It had been too good to be true. Gorgeous men did not stay by her side for long. There was always a more exciting, more beautiful woman waiting a few feet down the line.

"I am not abandoning you." His voice was sincere. "It is too dangerous for you to be with me."

"You're going to try and fight these Albireons."

"Yes." Eogan's voice was harsh. "They must be stopped. Soon they will be too strong to defeat."

"You can't possibly overthrow an organization like that alone."

"I will have my fellow Hunters with me." He shifted in his seat so that he was looking at her. "I cannot risk your life by taking you with me."

"What if I don't care?" Hester hated to beg, but she was at that point. "I came here to explore new ideas and now it's happening. It's unfair to leave me now."

He hesitated a second and then shook his head. "A Hunter's first duty is to make certain women are protected."

It felt as if the air had been emptied out of her balloon. She should be used to it by now. Romance happened to other women, not her. She had her studies and her career and that was more than enough for most people. That didn't keep her warm at night, though.

Buy a dog.

That's what her mother always told her.

This was the closest she'd ever come to an honest to goodness adventure, and she was lucky to be alive. Her fellow explorers were lying dead on the roadside. She was acting ungrateful and that had to stop. Tonight's exploits, and a pet, would have to hold her for the rest of her life.

"Take a right at the next intersection. My hotel is about a mile down the street."

Eogan turned back onto the road. "I did not mean to offend you."

"I'm used to it." She looked out of the window and watched the dimly lit streets go by. "I'm alive and I have you to thank for that."

"I can sense you're upset." Eogan's voice was soft. "I'm not deserting you. I am protecting you."

"You have rules and I understand." Hester sighed. Who was she kidding? She was disappointed and unhappy, and she had no right to be. "I came here to look at the ruin and to find out if UFO's and aliens were real."

"Then you have accomplished what you set out to do." He wheeled into the parking area for her hotel. "Your safety is important to me. I will search for you after the Albireons are overthrown if it is possible."

"Are you trying to tell me you might die?"

For the first time Hester considered the danger that Eogan might be walking into. He'd already told her that the combined effort of the world's governments might not be enough to defeat the Albireon threat. She was selfish and self-centered to only consider her problems.

"There are many Albireons and they have power on this planet." He stopped the car. "It will take a great many Hunters to destroy them."

"I hope you survive." She reached for the door knob. "Thank you for saving my life."

"Keep safe." His voice was low. "It might be best if you left Turkey immediately. I would hate to think that the Albireons and their allies have targeted you because you were with me."

Hester gulped. "I hadn't thought of that. I'll take the next plane out of the country. I don't care where it's going, I'll be on it."

It was a shame to relinquish her dreams, but necessary. There was no point in seeing ancient ruins if you didn't live long enough to tell others about it. Home had never looked so good or welcoming.

Eogan passed the backpack to her. "There will be a time when it is safe for you to return. Do not despair about these things."

Again he was reading her mind.

She reached for the pack and accidently touched his hand. A shiver of awareness raced through her body and settled like liquid heat in her inner core. She was headed for disappointment by letting herself be attracted to this guy, but she couldn't stop her body's reaction. She gave him a shaky smile and backed out of the car. The sooner she ended her connection with Eogan the better for her heart.

"Good luck."

He nodded and drove away.

She watched him leave until she lost sight of the jeep. It was probably the last time she'd see him so she lingered as long as possible. Hester shrugged and headed for her room. She was alive. That was more than the companions she'd set out with this evening. When she reached her room she threw the backpack on the bed and plopped down beside it. What a mess she'd made of her vacation. She'd have plenty of time to relive it later. Right now, she had to get herself out of this country as fast as possible.

What if someone had seen her leave with Steve or the others tonight? When the bodies of her companions were discovered, they would want to question her. What could she possibly say? I was attacked by some strange men and saved by an even stranger alien. That would get her locked up in a mental institution at the very least. For certain, her career at the university would be in jeopardy.

She couldn't risk the police questioning her.

The sooner she left Turkey, the safer she'd be.

Hester rolled off the bed and reached for the phone. She needed to call the airline and find a flight. She dialed the hotel switchboard and was waiting for an answer when there was an abrupt knocking at her door followed by the turning of the doorknob. Frowning, she looked to make certain she'd locked it. That's when the sound of something solid hitting the door filled the room.

The door shuddered.

Something hit it again.

Her heart stopped for a second and then started to beat at a frantic pace. Her eyes darted around the room looking for something to use as a weapon. There was nothing. She hefted her backpack in her hands. It was heavy enough to do damage. Wood splintered and then the door was kicked open.

Hester stood as if paralyzed.

Two men dressed in long black overcoats and black fedora hats entered the room.

"Put the phone down."

She shook her head.

One of the men snatched the receiver from her and slammed it back into its cradle. The other man grasped her arm and pulled her out of the room.

"You are coming with us."

Chapter 9

Eogan had driven only a couple of miles down the road before he regretted leaving the human woman alone. If he were being watched, they would know that she had helped him. That meant she was in danger. He stopped the jeep and took a deep breath. He had almost disobeyed the most important law of the sacred code.

Protect women and children.

To the death if necessary.

His actions may have put a woman in jeopardy. He had to remedy this situation and make certain she was safe before leaving to fight the Albireons. First, he had to contact the other Hunters. It was paramount that they knew he was free and what his plans were. If he died, then the others needed to continue his work.

He focused and sent out a message to the leader of the Hunter unit that was also stranded on this planet. Mind connect was a secret that only Hunters knew about. They could communicate telepathically. He had never met Ardal, who was Rioge clan. This would be the first time connecting and it might not be as easy as it would normally have been in battle.

"Ardal, this is Eogan."

It took several seconds and a couple of tries before he had a reply. *"I am listening."*

"Partlan advised me to contact you once I was above ground. I have escaped."

"Good. Where are you?"

"Sanliurfa,, Turkey. They tried to ambush me and have sent others to ensure that I am dead." Eogan tilted his head from side to side to ease the tension in his neck. *"My implants have been removed. They have no control over me."*

"I expected no less from a fellow Hunter." Ardal paused. *"Partlan and a team are in London. Can you get to them?"*

"I will make that my destination."

"I will alert them to your plans." There was a short pause before another mind connect message came through. *"It is good to know you are alive. We are the last of Rioge clan. I am anxious to meet with you and discuss the*

changes that have happened since landing on this planet."

"As am I."

"By Cygnus and Warrior make it to us safely."

That was the end of the connection.

Eogan had a destination and a purpose.

He was no longer a prisoner to the humans who wanted to control Earth. He was free to be the warrior and Hunter that he had been destined to be since his creation. It would be difficult to travel without papers, so he would have to stay away from the traditional means of transport. There was one thing he had to do before leaving this city and country.

Hester had risked her life by staying with him.

He had to be certain that she was safe.

He turned back in the direction of the hotel. The closer he got to where he'd left Hester, the tenser he became. It was an unusual sensation. He had never felt fear for himself. The only humans he'd known were those who held him captive or fought with him. He'd never cared about what happened to them.

It was different with Hester.

She had an effect on him.

The likeliest explanation was that it had been many years since he'd been close to another person. Isolation, and then the missions he'd been forced to perform, had taken away any real sense of belonging. He was alone and adrift from his fellow Hunters. Until he helped Partlan escape, he had no idea that any of his brother warriors had survived.

He slowed the jeep when the lodging came into sight.

His eyes narrowed when he noticed a new car in the parking lot. It was a large black sports utility vehicle. The humans that he'd worked with had driven identical vehicles. It was out of place in a small hotel on an isolated street. He parked and was about to open the door when two men came out of the building holding a woman between them.

It was Hester.

Eogan's heart raced and he fought back a surge of anger. He should never have left her alone. A wave of fear and distress knotted his stomach. It was so powerful that it took his breath away, and he knew without a doubt that it had come from Hester. She was terrified. The men pushed her into the SUV. There was only one option for him. He would follow the vehicle and when it stopped, he would free her.

He sent her a wave of strength.

She probably wouldn't be able to receive it, but he had to try. She needed to know that he was going to rescue her. He kept his lights off as he followed. They made their way through the city streets at a brisk pace, and drove north on the road to the airport. At the terminal, the vehicle turned away from the main buildings and continued to drive on a side street that ran parallel to the runways. It stopped past the runways at a gated, metal hangar.

There was a helicopter waiting on the tarmac.

It was a trap.

Somehow, they had found out that he'd travelled with Hester on his way back from Kobani. If they had followed him, then there must be another implant or tracking device on him. He didn't have time to worry about it right now.

He had to rescue Hester.

If possible, he would try and salvage the helicopter. It would be useful in their escape to London. He parked the jeep several yards away from the hangar and reached behind his seat for two assault rifles and a pistol. He checked the ammunition, swung the strap of one of the rifles over his shoulder, and pushed the handgun into his waistband.

He took a deep breath and calmed his heart beat. There was no room for error. He blocked all thought of Hester's fear from his mind and focused on his enemy. They must be eliminated. They had threatened a woman and only death would stop them. He eased the door of the jeep open and closed it with a quiet click.

A fence surrounded the helipad.

The gate was at the far end, so he kept low to the ground and crept toward the opening. He climbed the chain-link barrier and dropped down into the enclosure without detection. He used the building and the dark of night to hide his approach. The sports utility vehicle was stopped beside the helicopter, and as of yet, no one had exited.

They were waiting for him.

He crouched low to the ground and took aim.

He blasted out the tires of the SUV so that a hiss of escaping air echoed in the still night. He took aim, and ignited the fuel truck that was parked at the helipad. The loud boom of the explosion, and fire filled the area. The doors of the vehicle were flung open and a barrage of bullets volleyed up the side of the building that had hidden him.

Eogan's reactions were faster than the snipers. He'd left his initial position and was now behind a shed on the opposite side.

He shot two of the gunmen dead.

Only the driver, and probably one other person inside the car remained.

He was proved right a few seconds later. A man holding a gun to Hester's head, exited from the far side of the vehicle, and walked several feet onto the tarmac. The driver sped off. Eogan shot a barrage of bullets into the driver's side window. The SUV swerved out of control and crashed into the burning fuel truck.

"Enough," the man holding Hester, shouted. "There is no way you'll get out of here alive."

Eogan sprinted away from behind the shed and moved closer to Hester. Several wooden boxes that were lined up for transport, gave him cover. The overhead lights shone on Hester's abductor and Eogan had a clear shot from this vantage point. Soon the man would die.

"I was informed you were dead." The man shouted as he twirled in a circle holding Hester close to him. "You may have a reputation of being invincible, but no one is that good. Come out or the woman dies."

"Let her go first."

"I don't make deals with killers." The man snarled his words. "You will die this night. We no longer have a use for your expertise."

Eogan took aim.

He shot the man between the eyes.

Hester screamed as the man fell and took her with him. Eogan stood just as a blast rang out from the helicopter. The bullet flew within inches of his head. He had been so focused on saving Hester that he'd made the near-fatal error of thinking the chopper was empty. It was a rookie mistake.

The blades of the aircraft started, sending a gust of wind over the tarmac He crouched low and took aim. He was too late. The helicopter took off into the air. He rushed to Hester and watched the chopper leave with a sinking feeling.

She was trembling when he reached her side.

"Are you hurt?" His voice was curt.

Hester shook her head. "Is he dead?"

"You are safe."

Eogan freed her and then pulled her into his arms. He could feel the frantic racing of her heart against his chest. It felt as if his heart pulsed at the same rate. He sent her calming thoughts and within seconds, she had stopped shivering and her breathing returned to normal. Her fear was subsiding.

"We have to leave." Eogan looked down at her. "They'll send reinforcements. The helicopter pilot will have notified them."

Hester nodded and stood. "I thought they were going to kill me."

He picked up her backpack from the ground. "It was a trap. They knew that I would come to get you."

"How? Unless you were with me at the hotel, you would have had no way of knowing that they had kidnapped me."

Hester's logic made sense, but he was all too familiar with the Albireon methods. No matter how much they had tried to break him and force him to do their bidding, there was one thing he refused. He would never endanger or hurt a woman or child. His captors saw this as a weakness and used it to their advantage whenever possible.

"They intended to take you to a secure base. From there they would have made me aware that they had captured you."

"You're very familiar with their procedures." Hester's voice held a note of doubt.

"It is a strategy that they have employed before."

"And succeeded with?"

"Many times." Eogan took her arm and started to move her along the fence toward the gate. They still had a couple of hours of darkness and the sooner they were away from here, the safer it would be. Already he could hear the sirens of approaching fire suppression vehicles.

"They knew you were nearby." Hester reached a shaking hand for the door of the jeep. "That means they're still tracking you."

"I need to find the implant." Eogan slid behind the wheel of the car and turned the key in the ignition. "They must have injected one while I was being transported to Turkey."

"How will you find it?"

"It was probably inserted while I slept. The area I was kept in was gassed with a sleeping drug, so I never suspected."

Forced sleep was routine on a mission. There was always a fear that Eogan might try an escape, so they kept him subdued as much as possible. As hard as he fought it, he usually succumbed. He pointed the jeep toward the airport terminal.

"I may be able to use one of the security scanners that are employed on passengers to determine where it is."

"Then what?" Hester clutched her bag close to her chest.

"It will be lodged near a joint." It was a standard tracking device that all humans captured or working with the Albireons were injected with. "I will take it out."

"At this rate, you're going to be a mass of cuts before morning." Her voice was dry and a surge of relieve went through him. Her fear had subsided.

They drove to the terminal and parked. There were very few people around this early. He got out of the jeep and motioned for Hester to stay put.

"Not likely." Hester slammed her door shut. "The last time we separated two big men wearing black coats took me away. Where you go, I go."

"As you wish." Eogan felt a sensation of contentment settle over him. Having Hester beside him was comforting. He didn't understand why, but it would be easier to protect her if she was near.

There were only a couple of cleaning people in the terminal when they entered. It was still too early for passenger flights. He followed the signs for departures and assessed the security area. It was empty. Two uniformed guards were chatting by one of the closed airline kiosks.

Eogan shadowed one of the men when he moved away. He was probably going to walk his regular circuit, but he needed a scanner without causing a disturbance. The best way was to monitor the man until an opportunity presented itself. The guard went into a door marked security.

"We'll wait to see if he comes out." He motioned Hester to sit.

She pulled her backpack onto her lap. "The place might be full of guards."

"It is still too early for any flights." Eogan sat and crossed his arms over his chest. "That is probably the office and there should be scanners there."

"Can't you try and feel the implant?" Hester's voice was low. "That's what you did with the others."

"I knew where they were." Eogan rubbed his arm. "This was the device that the Kaladin gave me when I was created. The Albireons managed to redirect it so they could manipulate me. The one in my neck was implanted after I was captured. It had direct control over pain and whether I lived."

"That's horrible."

"That is how the Albireons operate." Eogan turned to her. "Did those men inject you with anything?"

Hester shook her head. "They grabbed me from the room and rushed me out before I could yell. In the car they were too concerned with keeping me quiet."

"You were screaming?" Eogan had assumed she'd been too terrified to do anything.

"I recited how many of my human rights they were violating." Hester shrugged. "It seemed to irritate them, so I maintained the litany until one of them threatened to gag me. By then, we had stopped and all hell broke out."

"I will still scan you just in case."

The guard left the room.

Eogan stood.

There were cameras everywhere and he had to get in quickly before they were spotted. Even though there were few people around, he couldn't take the chance that someone might be monitoring the feed. The Albireons and their security people would know where he was, but he and Hester would be gone before they could send another team to capture him.

"Do you have a cloth in that bag?"

Hester frowned. "Why?"

"I want to block that camera."

She rummaged through her backpack and pulled out a can of spray deodorant. "This might make everything fuzzy."

"That should give us enough time." Eogan took the can and walked up behind the camera. He sprayed the lens before ushering Hester into the office. It was empty. There were a couple of bookcases and one metal desk that was covered with papers and what looked to be the remains of someone's lunch. There were no scanners in sight. He started pulling out the drawers of the large bureau.

He found a hand-held scanner in the third drawer.

"This should tell me if there is any foreign material inside me." Eogan turned it on to the highest setting and then swiped it across his right arm.

Nothing happened.

He moved it down his right leg and up his left. Still the instrument made no noise. He switched hands and ran it across his left arm. It remained silent until it reached his wrist. It signaled that there was metal there. Eogan moved it several more times until he had narrowed the location of the chip.

"How did they get it in there?"

"They inject it into your bloodstream." Eogan put the detector on the desk. "It usually travels upstream. They had to have injected it when I was asleep so that might have affected where it traveled."

Hester opened her pack and pulled out the first aid kit. "Is it the same procedure as last time?"

Eogan nodded and held out his hand to her. "I will put pressure at the base of my wrist so the tracking device doesn't move. You cut it out."

She bit her lip. "Is this absolutely necessary?"

"If they find us, we are dead."

She took a deep breath and slit into his wrist below his thumb. There was blood and a second of pain before she started to probe inside his skin. A few twists and then a metal object was pushed out. She grabbed it and placed it on the desk.

Eogan applied pressure on the wound and waited while Hester put a bandage on the incision. Then he took the scanner and waved it over her body. She was clear. They hadn't had enough time to inject her with one of their tracking implants.

"We are free now." Eogan took the device and dropped it into a half-entry cup of coffee. It might still be transmitting, but the signal would be intermittent at best. He'd leave it here at the airport which should give them enough time to escape.

"Where do we go now?"

"We need to get out of this country." Eogan took her arm and opened the office door a few inches. The area was clear. "I have no papers so that makes air flight impossible."

"Next thing you'll be asking is if I know where to buy fake documents." Hester shook off his hand. "I don't, just in case you were wondering."

"I have connections."

"Since when?" Hester's voice was doubtful. "I think our best bet is to blend in with the local populace. Maybe we could pretend to be refugee's and try to escape that way."

"Why would they believe us?"

Hester gave him a quick glance. "I could cover my hair and face, but you'd stand out. They'd be no disguising that you're not Syrian."

"I am a Hunter." Eogan didn't understand Hester's words. A Hunter did not hide who he was. "We need to leave, now."

"I was just trying to come up with an escape plan." Her voice was filled with exasperation. "There are a lot of refugees in this part of the world. This could work to our advantage."

"True." Eogan liked the idea, but they would never blend in successfully. "The borders will be watched, but we can copy the same methods that some refugees use to leave Turkey."

"Quite a large number are arriving in Europe by boat. They must be hiring people to take them."

"Then we must get to the ocean." Eogan looked around the airport parking lot. "We cannot take the jeep. They know we are in it and will track it."

"Don't ask me to steal." Hester crossed her arms.

"I won't." There was a fire orange glow on the horizon as the sun rose. Eogan noticed the car rental kiosks and headed toward them. An attendant was just opening up his office. "Do you have money?"

Chapter 10

Thirty minutes later, they were driving west toward Iskenderun. It was the nearest port and they could probably rent a boat there to get them out of the country. Hester's head was still spinning from all that had happened in the past few hours. She had certainly got the adventure she'd craved. Kidnapping, murder, archaeological ruins, and a hunky rescuer.

It was more than she'd expected.

A shiver of awareness went through her as she glanced over at Eogan.

Lean muscles rippled up his arm as he gripped the steering wheel. She was traveling with a man who was utterly gorgeous. Yesterday, when she woke up, the most she'd hoped from the day was that she'd get to examine Gobekli Tepe undisturbed. She loved everything ancient, but it was no comparison to having a real live man sitting beside her.

The car braked and Eogan turned off the road.

"What's wrong?" Hester expected the worse. She couldn't help it. After everything that had happened, it was a reasonable assumption.

"We need to disable the tracking device."

"Not another one?" Where did this guy keep coming up with these things? "You scanned both of us. We're clear."

"Not us. The car."

Eogan pushed his seat back and started to feel under the dash. He pulled open what looked like a fuse box. He poked around the wires and then snapped the cover back on. "It's not here."

"Why would a leased car have a tracking device?"

"To prevent theft."

"We paid for it." She wondered if captivity had addled his brain. "They have my credit card number on file. They'll just charge me if they don't get it back."

"Most rental companies monitor their cars."

Hester shook her head. "That's an invasion of my rights."

Eogan raised an eyebrow. "No one has privacy."

She opened her mouth and then shut it. He was right. Monitoring, whether by camera, internet, or RFID chips was everywhere. Who was she to argue? If last night had taught her anything, it was that she didn't have a clue as to what was happening in the real world. She'd spent too much time among musty old books and artifacts.

"Where would they put it?"

"Usually it's plugged into the onboard computer system of the car. This organization took it a step further and hid it."

Hester groaned. She didn't want to walk all the way to the coast. "Does that mean we can't use the vehicle?"

Eogan reached below the dash and the hood of the car popped up. "No. I just have to look in a different location."

There was no doubt that Eogan was determined. He was also very knowledgeable. If it hadn't been for him, she would have been lying dead by the side of the road. So much for all the reading and research she'd done on the internet before heading out on her adventure. She didn't even know the basics about renting a car.

Hester sighed. There was nothing she could do about what had happened now. The first priority was to get out of this country alive. Once she was back home and safe, she could look at this whole escapade in a new light. She'd also widen her research topics to include tips on traveling.

Eogan slammed the hood down.

He was holding a black box in his hand.

"Is that it?"

He nodded. "I'm going to leave it here. They'll think we've stopped to sightsee. It shouldn't raise any alarms for a few hours."

"This is going to ruin my credit rating." Hester felt as if she were on a roller coaster. "Do you think we'll be safe in Iskenderun?"

"We will not be out of danger until I can reach the other Hunters."

"They know you're coming?"

"I've contacted them. We are to meet in London."

"When did you have time?" Hester's eyes widened. "Do you have a cellphone? They could be tracking that."

"I don't need such a device to contact my brothers." Eogan spun the car back onto the road.

"You probably have some unique system to communicate." Hester didn't bother to hide her sarcasm. "You guys sound more like superheroes. It must be nice to land on a new world and have super powers."

"I do not have special abilities." Eogan glanced at her. "This planet gives me some advantages, but as you have seen I bleed, and I can still be controlled."

A wave of regret washed through her. She'd been callous, and the worse thing he'd done was save her life twice. Even if he was an alien, he deserved more respect than that. He had risked his life when he could have left her to fend for herself.

Hester leaned her head against the headrest. "I was out of line."

"We are not following a line." Eogan sounded confused. "You speak in riddles again."

"You don't seem to understand English very well. Is it a second language for you?"

"It is one of the dialects that was downloaded when I crashed."

"Are you certain you've been here thirty years? You sound as if you arrived here yesterday."

"I do not lie."

Hester snorted. "I remember. I suppose being locked away has kept you from mingling with others. You seem to do everything better than the rest of us, except understand the nuances of the language."

"The people who held me captive did not care about how I spoke." Eogan's voice was dry. "This planet has given me several advantages. I heal quickly and age slower."

"Too bad you couldn't bottle that and sell it. You'd make a fortune."

Hester turned to look out the window. The sun was up and the sky was a brilliant blue. The area they were passing through was flat with grass and sparse vegetation. In the distance there was a low mountain range and the outline of another city. She hadn't considered the scenery of Turkey because she was focused only on seeing Gobekli Tepe.

"This is a beautiful country, but I suppose you've seen it before." She looked over at Eogan.

"Never in daylight."

"That's unbelievable." Hester shook her head. "Didn't they let you out during the day?"

"Sometimes." Eogan's voice was matter of fact. "Most of my assignments were at night."

"How does Earth compare with your home planet?"

"It is an oasis compared to Cygnus." Eogan kept his eyes on the road. "You have trees and water still. It would be a shame to see this destroyed."

Hester was intrigued. She believed there were other planets where life thrived, but how they looked had never crossed her mind. The snippets of information she was finding out about Eogan were an anthropological goldmine. He was a giant of a man, with a powerful presence. A skilled killer who lived by a code of honor.

Every moment she spent with him was a risk to her life because he was an alien hunted by a secret government agency. None of that mattered when she looked into his dark eyes. All she wanted to do was drown in those eyes and forget the rest of the world. It was crazy. And it had to stop.

Men didn't notice her, especially if they looked like Eogan. The only place this could lead to was heartbreak. She had to end this insane attraction to a man who was unattainable. Focusing on the academics of this situation would clear her mind and protect her heart.

"Did the Albireons destroy your planet too?"

"They would never dare." His voice was a growl. "The ancients left Cygnus barren thousands of years ago."

"If you can travel in space, you must have the technology to restore your homeland."

"It is not easy to replace what is gone. We may have the ability to store and manipulate genes, but some things do not return."

"Like water and plants?"

Eogan nodded. "We have artificial water and areas where trees have been preserved, but it is not the same. It's easier to find new planets to inhabit."

"That's tragic." A wave of sadness filled Hester. They were close to destroying the environment on Earth, but there wasn't another planet for humans to populate. "What else is different?"

"I have found many strange things on this world. The most difficult adjustment was discovering that not all humans tell the truth."

"Don't try and tell me that all people from your world speak honestly." Hester shook her head. "Nobody is that perfect."

"Hunters do not lie. It is against our sacred code."

"If you assume all Hunters are truthful, you would never know if they lied."

"It would bring dishonor."

"And that's a great sin for you?"

"A Hunter lives and dies by honor."

"The only people I truly trust are my parents."

"That is why I have to ask about the men you were traveling with to Gobekli Tepe." Eogan's voice was low. "When did you meet them?"

"I'd only met them in person yesterday afternoon. I'd spoken to Steve many times on the internet."

"Were these communications monitored?"

Hester frowned. "What are you suggesting?"

"What were these men hoping to find at Gobekli Tepe?"

"They wanted to prove that the ruin was connected with extraterrestrials who had visited this planet in our distant past."

"And you accepted this explanation for their trip?" He looked at her with a raised eyebrow.

"Of course. It's the reason all of us were there." Hester's voice rose with indignation. "That's why I came to Turkey. I needed to see the carvings on the stones."

"So you risked going with strangers?"

"Steve and I had communicated for over a year before I decided to come here. He wasn't a complete stranger." Hester understood Eogan's hesitation to believe Steve's intentions, but academics frequently corresponded by email for years without meeting.

"You don't know what his agenda was."

"He wanted the same thing that I did." She didn't bother to hide her exasperation. "When I met him yesterday he was exactly as I had envisioned. He was a wealth of information about Gobekli Tepe. He'd visited it many times. I wasn't about to complain when he wanted other people to join us."

"You were almost killed." Eogan's tone was critical. "They left you to defend yourself and that tells me they can't be trusted."

"Three of them did die." Hester shivered as she remembered the horror of the previous night. "I can't blame Steve and Franklin for saving themselves."

"If we're traveling together you must trust me and do what I ask." He gave her a sharp look. "That's the only way I can protect you."

"I've fended for myself for thirty years. Nobody is going to dictate how I act." She wasn't about to relinquish her independence for any man, even if she found him attractive.

"Hunters do not give women orders unless it involves safety," Eogan said. "Your protection is all that concerns me."

"You seem very quick to tell me what I can and cannot do." Hester crossed her arms. "I'm capable of choosing my friends without your interference."

"I caution that you don't know these men as well as you think. The ambush that you were caught in may not have been about me. What if they were really looking for your companions?"

A shiver of fear went through Hester. She hadn't given any thought as to why those men had been waiting for them on the road. The other strange thing was that Steve and Franklin had been so quick to drive away. They hadn't looked back or hesitated.

"You said they were looking for you."

"I've had time to reconsider what happened." He frowned. "There is no doubt that I was being tracked, but they couldn't have known in advance what direction I would take. You said those men ambushed you."

"So you think they were after Steve all along?"

"You may have triggered a security breach by all of your investigations into aliens."

"Most people consider us crazy, and ignore everything we say."

Eogan gripped the steering wheel tighter. "Everything on the Internet and the telephone is monitored. Any talk of extraterrestrial beings will be flagged."

"I'm an archaeologist who teaches at a small Midwestern University. Why would anyone care what I say?"

"You were discussing the possibility that aliens had been on this planet. The Albireons, who are extraterrestrials, control the world's economy and resources. They have been on earth for the past seventy years."

"We were just speculating about other life forms. Steve has been involved with UFO research for years. Why would anyone decided that he is a risk all of a sudden?"

"What do you know about Franklin?"

"He was Steve's friend. It was the first time I had ever met him." Hester frowned. "He was more intense than Steve or the others. Whenever he spoke, it sounded like he was giving us military instructions."

"What kind of directions?" Eogan eased the speed of the car.

"He talked about being on the lookout for the enemy and being certain to protect our flank." She shrugged. "To be honest I didn't pay much attention."

"It sounds as if he was expecting trouble."

"How could that be possible?" Hester turned in her seat to look at Eogan. "As far as I knew, we only planned to go to Gobekli Tepe."

"His agenda may have been different." His voice was dry. "He might have suspected that you were being followed."

"So he led us into the trap?" Hester didn't bother to hide her doubt.

"I'm concerned that they kidnapped you at the hotel. How did they know you were with me? At no time did anyone see us together."

Hester inhaled a sharp breath. "They knew I was there."

"Either that, or they were waiting in case you returned." His words sent a shiver of dread up her spine.

"You think they've been watching me?"

"Probably." He stepped on the accelerator. "The sooner we get you to safety, the better. Can you recall any details about the others?"

Hester shivered. She suddenly had a new perspective on how it felt to be hunted. Before, she'd been worried about Eogan, but it had been his reality, not hers. Now she wasn't so sure. Eogan had raised a few points that troubled her. She tried to concentrate and remember yesterday's meeting with the men at the café.

"No one was nervous." Hester rubbed her forehead. "It was a carefree discussion about ancient monoliths and what the possible meanings could be."

"Was Franklin there too?"

Hester's eyes widened. "He joined us later."

"That was the first time you saw him?"

Hester nodded. "Josh didn't know him either. It was Steve who vouched for him. After all, Franklin was providing the van. We weren't in any position to tell him that he couldn't join us."

"Did he say anything that seemed out of place?"

Hester shrugged. "We were all talking about some pretty strange stuff. Most people would think it was all out of place."

Eogan's jaw tightened. "Did he do anything differently? I'm looking for a clue as to who he was working for."

"You think he's a spy?"

"It is possible." He slowed the vehicle down before turning onto the road to Iskenderun.

Hester sensed his frustration. She tried to focus on the conversation that had taken place the previous day, but it was hopeless. Fear and stress had pushed everything away except the fact that she was running for her life, and trying to get out of Turkey. She crossed her arms and leaned her head back.

Who was she kidding?

Sitting beside Eogan was making it nearly impossible to think. It was as if the essence of his being was reaching out to her. All she wanted was to have this feeling continue. It made no difference that they were on the run, or had tampered with a rental vehicle. All that mattered was that Eogan was with her.

A fleeting memory drifted through her mind.

She frowned as she considered the conversation. It had seemed strange at the time, and now in hindsight, it was even more significant. Franklin had been speaking to Steve in a hushed tone when she had first arrived at the van. They had stopped immediately after they saw her, but not before she'd heard what they were saying.

"Franklin was talking about some organization that he called H.R.F."

Chapter 11

It was a term that Eogan was not familiar with. That didn't mean he could ignore it. He had to be certain that Hester wasn't being pursued by this organization. Any information that he could gather about the group would help him protect her. Her safety was the most important thing right now. He'd worry about getting to the other Hunters after he knew she was out of danger.

"What does that mean?" He looked over at Hester. "I have not heard anything about H.R.F. before."

"Neither had I. That's why I thought it was strange."

"When did he mention it?"

"He was talking to Steve, and they didn't realized that I was standing by the van." Hester's voice was reflective. "He said the H.R.F. was prepared to do battle. That's why I thought he was a military person."

"Did they say what kind of combat?"

"They were discussing conspiracy theories and how they were all ready for an invasion." Hester shrugged. "It just sounded like the usual Ufologist rhetoric. In the chat rooms, they're always talking about alien abductions and how unprepared we are for an attack."

"So you think this group is part of the plan to stop such an assault."

"They could be. I didn't hear much more because once they saw me, they turned the conversation to Gobekli Tepe and the possible meaning of the carvings on the stones."

Eogan frowned. He'd been held a prisoner below ground for the past six months so anything could have happened in that time. He needed to know if the other Hunters were aware of this group. His other concern was whether this H.R.F. should be trusted or feared.

"We'll be in Iskenderun in an hour." He looked at Hester. Fatigue and weariness were written all over her face. "Sleep. I'll wake you when we arrive."

She nodded and leaned her head against the window of the passenger side. Eogan forced himself to look away. She looked beautiful and at peace with her arms crossed over her bag and her glasses slipping down her nose. Never had he noticed a woman before, and for a few seconds he let himself savor the sensation of attraction that ripped through his body as he gazed at her.

It was intoxicating.

It was addictive.

He was a warrior and women had no place in his life. It was forbidden for a Hunter to mate on his home planet. Partlan had told him that being on Earth and removing their implants had meant that some Hunters had found their pair bonds and mates. He hadn't believed it could happen to him, though.

Hester was the first woman he'd met after he'd pulled out his Kaladin implant. It was incredible that he could bond with anyone that quickly. A part of him wanted to deny what was happening, but the longer he stayed with her, the deeper his connection was growing. There was no denying the attraction he felt for her.

He needed to find out if this conversation that Hester had overheard was the reason she might be targeted. If they were on the run from two different organizations then he would change his strategy. He'd assumed that the Albireons were the only ones after them. It was their men that had tried to kidnap Hester.

Now he needed to find out about this H.R.F.

He sent out a mind connect to Ardal. "*I am headed toward Iskenderun.*"

"*How long before you reach it?*"

"*An hour or less.*" Eogan glanced over at Hester who was still sleeping. "*I will have company. We intend to rent a boat and head for Cypress.*"

"*I will see if there is a team close by.*"

"*Another complication has arisen. We have run into an organization called H.R.F. and they may be pursuing us.*"

"*I have not heard of them.*" There was a second of hesitation before Ardal connected again. "*I will have my men search for any information concerning them.*"

"*I will let you know when we are in Cypress.*"

"*Stay alert.*"

"*Always.*"

Eogan ended the mind connect. Ardal's men should be able to tell him shortly if there was going to be a problem with H.R.F. A surge of determination rushed through him. There was no way he was going to let anyone hurt Hester. She may have stumbled into a plot that she had no knowledge of. It was his responsibility to ensure that she survived without harm.

They were entering the outskirts of Iskenderun when Hester yawned and stretched her arms over her head. A sense of calm and peace came over Eogan at the sight of her awake. He kept his eyes on the road as he maneuvered through the busy streets on his way to the harbor and waited until she was fully conscious.

"This is a beautiful city." Hester's voice was filled with awe. "No wonder they call this the Turquoise Coastline."

"We should reach the port in a few minutes."

"Good." Hester shifted in her seat. "I need to stretch my legs."

"You must stay near." Alarm raced through him. "I can't risk you getting lost or taken."

"I'll keep close." Hester waved away his objections. "You'll have to do all of the negotiations for the boat. I don't speak the language."

The harbor came into view and Eogan slowed so that he could park the car. They locked the vehicle and then walked along the pier looking at the boats available for rent. Most were small and wouldn't be able to do the crossing that they wanted. When they had reached the end of the dock they found a larger boat in need of paint. There was an older man standing on its deck and he waved them closer.

"We need to go a distance." Eogan looked at the ship.

"She will go as far as you can pay." The man spoke in broken English.

"Great," Hester said under her breath. "I don't have much cash left."

"How much for Cypress?" Eogan watched the man's face as he considered the request.

"Seven hundred lira each."

"How many American dollars is that?" she asked.

"I will take both of you for five hundred US dollars." The man crossed his arms over his chest.

Hester went to open her backpack.

Eogan put his hand over hers. "Two hundred."

He began the negotiations. He had learned this technique when he'd been stranded with other soldiers after finishing a mission. As per protocol, there was no exit strategy for the team. They'd bartered a lower price. When Eogan had questioned it, they'd advised him that they would be less memorable if they behaved as regular tourists. He also didn't want Hester spending all of her money. It might be necessary later.

"That is too little. I need to pay for my fuel." The captain waved away his suggestion.

Eogan crossed his arms and waited.

It took a couple of seconds before the man made a counteroffer. "Three hundred."

Eogan glanced at Hester, and she nodded. "It is agreed."

They boarded the ship. Hester handed over the money, and they found a place at the front of the boat. There was a short delay while the captain cast off. The morning was brisk and the breeze was a pleasant respite. Eogan had spent six months underground, and the scenic coastline and majestic mountain range that framed the port were a welcomed sight. He relaxed the tension in his body. Soon they would be free of this place.

Hester leaned against him.

A jolt of electricity went through him.

A quick inhale of breath from Hester told him that she'd felt it too. She looked toward the disappearing harbor and rubbed her arm. He sensed her uncertainty and reluctance to speak about what was happening between them. He didn't quite understand it either, but to keep silent was wrong.

"There is a connection between us." He spoke his thoughts aloud.

Hester's eyes widened. "There's no way that you could be feeling anything toward me. I appreciate that you're trying not to hurt my feelings. I feel like a fool."

"Why?"

"Somehow, you've guessed that I'm attracted to you." Hester shrugged. "What woman wouldn't be? You're gorgeous and very protective."

"No woman has ever noticed me before."

"I find that impossible to believe." Hester's eyebrow rose. "You could have your pick of any woman. No man wants me."

"That's not true." He had to convince her that he was drawn to her. "You are very beautiful."

"You told me before that you weren't interested in women." Hester pushed her glasses up her nose. "I gave up the dream of finding a man long ago. You don't have to spare my feelings. It's very gallant of you to try and ease my embarrassment."

"I do not lie." Eogan clenched his hands tight onto the side of the boat. He was handling this badly. "I want to explain to you about Hunters."

"You're warriors and not from this planet. What else is there to know?"

"We are not like other men."

"I gathered that." Hester's voice was dry.

Eogan turned to her. "Women are forbidden to Hunters."

Hester frowned. "What do you mean?"

"We do not have mates."

"Never?"

He shook his head. "Our implants make it impossible."

She glanced down at his forearm. "They stopped you from being attracted to women?"

"Because of the genetic modifications that have been done to us through the ages, we are devoted and fierce warriors. We obey orders and die with honor. We are the perfect soldier and the Kaladin did not want to risk anything interfering with that."

"They thought that having a mate would distract you?" Hester's voice rose in indignation. "That's crazy. Men and women have spouses and families and still make good soldiers."

"On Earth. Not in Cygnus." Eogan lowered his voice. "You forget that our genes have been changed. At one time, the Kaladin allowed us to bond until they found out how different we were from other men."

"That sounds ominous." Hester's gaze didn't leave his face. "What happened?"

"We form pair bonds that last a lifetime and are so intense that nothing can sever it. There is only one mate for a Hunter and not even death can dissolve the connection or change its importance."

Her eyes widened. "You never want anyone else, not even if your partner dies?"

"Never." Eogan took her hand in his. "There are secrets that Hunters have among themselves. Not even the Kaladin are aware of them."

Hester's hand twitched in his. "Do they involve your mate?"

Eogan nodded. "We are connected to our pair bond on every level. Mentally, emotionally, and physically. If she is in trouble we will do everything in our power to protect her and that includes disobeying orders."

"So the Kaladin didn't want to risk that happening." Hester bit her lower lip. "That still seems unfair to deny you the chance to have a family."

"We were designed to be warriors, nothing else." Eogan spoke in a dispassionate voice.

He had never considered what had been done to him as wrong. His sole purpose was to fight and die. It was his honor to do that for the Kaladin. Since coming to Earth, and being forced to do the bidding of the Albireons, he had altered his thinking. He wasn't certain that a Hunter only had one purpose in life. There had to be more. Now that his implants had been removed, he was realizing that he'd been right.

"It must have been hard being denied a family and wife." Hester's voice was full of sympathy.

"We didn't believe it was possible for us to mate." Eogan looked out over the ocean. He still didn't fully trust what was happening. "Until we crashed landed on Earth, the idea of a pair bond and mate was only a legend."

"How did that change?"

"The other Hunters who are stranded here, have removed their implants. They have discovered that it is possible to have a mate." Eogan looked back at Hester. "They have even found that they can have children."

"That's impossible. You're not from Earth."

"We carry the same genes as humans."

For a few seconds Hester was silent. Eogan sensed the emotions and questions that were going through her. He knew it shouldn't be possible and yet it was happening. Hester's thoughts were beginning to become his. There was only one explanation for that and the idea was incredible.

"That can only mean one of two things. Either humans come from a different planet and were brought here while you were left on Cygnus."

"Or Hunters were taken from Earth by the Kaladin and altered." Eogan finished the thought for her.

"Which was it?"

"We are unsure."

Hester's eyes widened. "You know this proves the theory that extraterrestrials were on this planet in the past. Steve would love to hear this."

"This is not for the ears of your friends."

"I understand, but it's still pretty cool." Hester sighed. "To think that we were right about aliens visiting Earth."

"They are still here."

Hester nodded. "I remember. The Albireons are trying to take over the world."

"I do not consider it lightly." Eogan's voice was stern. "I have had to work for them for the last thirty years. They have controlled my actions, thoughts, and body. They are very real."

Hester swallowed. "When you put it like that, it's very ominous."

"Our situation will not be safe until we have joined the other Hunter units." Eogan's grip on Hester's hand tightened. "I cannot allow anything to happen to you."

Hester nodded. "I appreciate that you feel obligated to protect me, but you should think about yourself first. You are in greater danger than me."

"You don't understand." Eogan cleared his throat. "The reason I told you about Hunters and pair bonds was because I sense that I am bonding with you."

Hester stared at him with unblinking eyes. "That's impossible. No man wants me."

"I desire you very much."

She shook her head. "That's just because I was the first woman you saw after your implants were removed. It's a response to having freedom from controls."

"I have explained this wrong." Eogan leaned closer to her and the scent of her skin twirled around his nostrils sending his body into a spin of reaction. "If I have bonded with you, there will never be another woman."

Hester shook her head. "I'm not the type of woman who inspires that kind of devotion. Men never look my way. I'm plain and overweight. I keep my nose buried in books during the day, and at night, I chat with others on the internet."

"That is not what I see when I look at you." Eogan knew he had to pick his words carefully. "I see the woman that I am destined to be connected with. I understand that you aren't attracted to me, and I would never force you into something you did not desire. Whether we ever mate or not, you will always be the one I am bonded to."

Just then the boat slowed down. They had left the harbor long ago and were headed out into open water. Eogan watched as the captain stepped away from the steering wheel. He walked toward them and motioned down. "You should go below."

"We will do that shortly." Hester smiled at the man. "Right now it's wonderful to get some fresh air."

The captain shrugged. "It is safer in the galley."

Eogan's eyes narrowed and he scanned the horizon. Although there was nothing in sight, he didn't like the tone of the captain's voice. The man seemed to be hinting at danger. Before they could move, his ears picked up the faint sound of an engine. There was nothing in the water. That meant it had to be in the air.

"We need to go below."

Hester must have sensed the urgency in his voice. She stood, and let him lead her to the ladder. He motioned for her to go first. Once she was safe, he started down the ladder, followed by the captain. Eogan stopped so that he was able to see what was happening above. The sound of the engine grew louder.

It was a helicopter.

Chapter 12

Hester could hear the whirring of the chopper's blades as it circled the boat. A shiver of dread raced up her spine. Logically, she knew they were safe. Eogan had pulled out all of the tracking devices inside of him and then scanned both of them to be certain. This must be just a routine flyby.

Eogan grabbed the captain by his shirt. "Did you notify someone?"

The captain took a step backwards and fell on the lower deck. "It is standard practice to let the harbor know where the boat is going in case of emergency."

"Is it normal to have them fly so close for an inspection?"

The captain shook his head. "It is very unusual."

Eogan crossed his arms. "They will think it is suspicious if we're all below deck."

The captain stood. "They are looking for boats that are carrying refugees. It is obvious that we are too small for that."

Hester pulled her bag closer. She needed the comfort of something familiar and this was the closest thing she had left from her life back home. Her father had given her the leather backpack when she'd earned her first degree. Everything else she had brought with her was abandoned in the hotel in Sanliurfa. She shivered as she remembered the men who had abducted her from her room. She was thankful she wouldn't have to meet them again.

"You are safe." Eogan spoke in a reassuring voice. "Even if others come for us, I will protect you."

A wave of calm raced through her, and Hester took a deep breath. Eogan was right. There was nothing to worry about. He had killed the other men and this helicopter inspection was probably a check for refugees. Once they were clear of any wrongdoing, they'd be free to continue their journey.

A few seconds later, the aircraft turned away.

Hester shivered with reaction.

"They are leaving." The captain went up the ladder. "It was a random visual inspection."

"Thank goodness."

She leaned back against the side of the vessel. She was sitting in what looked to be a galley area with a sink, burner, and ice cabinet. It was primitive. Hopefully they'd reach Cypress before they had to make use of it. The engine of the boat revved and they returned to the rapid pace that they'd been moving at before the surveillance helicopter.

"We should be safe now." She gave Eogan weak smile. "It was foolish of me to be so upset."

He shook his head. "There is something not right about this."

Hester was on alert again. "What is it? We know that we aren't being tracked, and the captain seems to be telling the truth."

"I do not trust him." Eogan clenched his fists. "We should leave this boat."

"Are you crazy? We're in the middle of the ocean."

"He must have a lifeboat." Eogan started up the stairs. "The longer we stay, the greater the risk."

She rolled her eyes. "I think you're paranoid."

"I have to keep you safe." Eogan disappeared above deck.

Hester closed her eyes and counted to ten. They had passed the helicopter surveillance and still Eogan didn't trust it. It had been an insane plan to try and charter a boat to take them to Cypress, and yet at the time, it had seemed the easiest way to escape Turkey.

Now that they were out of the country, and free of the men who'd been pursuing them, they should be able to relax. She didn't think that was possible for a man like Eogan. Then again, he wasn't like normal men. He was from another planet.

She shook her head as she remembered the conversation that they'd been having before the helicopter arrived. He'd actually told her he was attracted to her. A shiver of pleasure raced through her. To know that what she was feeling for him might be returned was in the realm of fairy tales, and she'd given up on those a long time ago.

When she was young, she'd often dreamed about the man who would be the other half of her. Time and reality had dashed those dreams. Instead of marriage, she'd become an independent woman of letters. Academia had replaced the emptiness in her heart, and even though it was a cold bedfellow, it didn't disappoint.

Disillusionment had happened at her first high school social. She'd been left standing at the wall while all the other girls had been asked to dance. The new outfit and dancing lessons had gone to waste that night, but she'd learned a valuable lesson. It was the pretty girls who got asked out, not the nerdy girls in glasses. She had a choice to make. Either she could throw herself into trying to be something she wasn't or she could focus on other things.

Archaeology was her selection.

She'd never regretted her decision.

Hester excelled in school and had earned her doctorate by the time she was twenty-five. She might not have tenure at the university, but she was respected in her field and enjoyed teaching. It was also boring and mundane. That's why she'd been researching extraterrestrials visiting Earth. It was exciting and definitely breaking the rules of academia

Now, she had a gorgeous, hunk of a man, telling her he found her attractive.

She needed to pinch herself because this had to be a dream.

It is a pair bonding for life. She swore she heard Eogan's voice in her head. She gave herself a shake and stood. It was times she got some fresh air. She had reached the ladder when another sound caught her attention.

She poked her head above board. "What is that?"

"It looks like a Coast Guard cutter." Eogan turned to her. "Hide below. If it is me they want then they will not find you."

"I can't let you be taken. You said they want you dead."

"I will escape." Eogan's voice was insistent. "It's better if you are safe. I can defeat them and return to you when I am free."

"You say that like it's an easy thing."

Hester debated about listening to him, but the roar of a horn convinced her. They were saying something over a loudspeaker in several languages. When they spoke in English, it was clear what their intentions were.

"Prepare to be boarded."

"Get out of sight." Eogan's voice was barely audible.

Hester backed down the ladder and moved into the cluttered rear of the boat. It was more of a storage closet than a room. She pushed under a number of empty boxes and tucked her head out of sight. There was nowhere else to hide.

Footsteps sounding above.

Shouts and then the screams of the captain.

Hester's body shook. Her imagination was vivid enough that it was filling in the details of what was happening with all of the worst case scenarios. She should be up there with Eogan. He was going to be captured, and she would never see him again. It was just her luck to finally find a man who might be interested in her and she'd lose him on the high seas.

The blast of a gun ripped through the air.

Hester's breath caught in her throat. Footsteps sounded over the whole ship. There was a man shouting questions and then there was the sound of someone being hit.

Dread filled her.

Was Eogan hurt?

What were the men looking for? Surely if they had Eogan that was what they had come for. Her body shook. She was trapped here and there was nothing she could do except pray that Eogan was fine.

She strained to hear the words of a low murmured conversation. She didn't understand the language. Another few seconds of silence were followed by more pounding of feet on the ship's floor boards. This time they were headed toward the door that led below deck.

She heard heavy boots on the ladder.

They were coming for her.

She tried to back up against the side of the boat, but she was as close to it as possible. She inhaled and brought her arms and legs closer in an attempt to make herself smaller. The footsteps were near. Boxes were thrown out of the way and then hands were reaching for her.

They grabbed her hair.

She was yanked upright.

The man holding her had an ugly smirk on his face. "You cannot hide from us."

He clutched her arm and pushed her ahead of him, forcing her up the stairs. The bright sunshine brought tears to her eyes and she had to blink until she could adjust to the light. What she saw sent her heart beating at a furious pace.

The captain was wounded and lying face down on the deck.

Eogan was on his knees and his hands were bound behind his back.

"Bring her here." A heavy-set man in military uniform barked. He wore the insignia of colonel and a tag with the name Schneider.

Hester was pushed until she stood in front of the man. He had short gray hair, and beady eyes, which bore into her. She forced herself to stand tall, and straightened her shoulders. She wasn't going to let this man intimidate her.

"You've led us on a merry chase." The man's voice was deep and threatening. "I've lost good men because of you."

Confusion filled her as she looked from the man speaking to her, and then to Eogan. Eogan's face was impassive, his eyes downcast as if he were contemplating the boat deck. Beside him, the captain was moaning and holding his leg. The man who had brought her above grasped her arm and pulled her toward the edge.

"Where she goes, I go." Eogan's voice was a low threat.

The man in charge looked at him and laughed. "Do you honestly think you're in a position to stop us?"

"Yes."

A chill went through Hester. Instinctively, she knew that Eogan was going to kill all of them. She steadied her breathing and tensed her muscles in preparation. After seeing him in action, she had no doubt that he would defeat these men. The man in charge must have sensed the same thing.

Colonel Schneider grasped her close and put a pistol to her throat. "Alright, big guy. When you're screaming for freedom, don't forget that I was willing to let you go."

"It will not come to that." Eogan stood. "If you harm her, I will rip you apart with my bare hands."

The colonel smirked. "Big words for a man in restraints. Because you're so eager you can go first."

Eogan walked by them.

The colonel brought the butt of his pistol down on Eogan's head, sending him sprawling across the deck. "Pick him up, boys, and throw him into the hold."

Hester opened her mouth to speak, but the colonel tightened his fingers around her neck. "One word out of you, missy, and you'll be shark bait. I don't care what the brass say they want. Do you understand?"

She nodded.

He loosened his grip, and she took a shaky breath. She didn't know what these people wanted with her. She was an archaeologist, not a terrorist, yet she was being treated like a criminal. She was taken off the boat and hauled into the larger ship that had stopped them. It was equipped with guns mounted on its sides and top.

They'd sent the heavy artillery for her.

She'd never been a threat to anyone.

She didn't have a clue as to what she could have possibly done to make these people so angry. She'd have to wait to get an explanation. They threw her into the hole beside Eogan. He was sprawled out on his stomach in the corner.

He'd risked his life to be with her. No man had ever noticed her enough to help her. Gratitude and the warm glow of love burst inside of her. She'd probably regret giving her heart away so quickly, yet there was no denying that she was falling in love with Eogan. He was everything she'd ever dreamed of in a man.

He was protective, honorable, sincere, and most of all, he'd proven that he wanted to be with her. There were no recriminations or judgements from Eogan. Instead, he'd risked his life again to be with her. She'd been a fool to get herself into this situation, and she didn't even know what she was involved in.

She rushed to his side and checked the back of his head, before untying his hands.

He groaned.

"Can you hear me?" She tried to turn him over so she could see his face. He was like a lead weight. "How much do you weigh?"

"Enough." Eogan moaned and turned onto his back. He brought a hand up to his head and winced. "I should not have angered him, but there was no other way to stay with you. There were too many weapons aimed at the boat for me to risk attacking them. You might have been hurt."

She sat back on the floor. "I don't understand why they want me. It was you they were following."

"That is what I thought." He reached for the leather backpack that was still clutched in Hester's hands. "We need to dump that out."

"You think they put something in here?" Hester shook her head. "It is never out of my sight."

"Nevertheless, we must check. It is the last possible place that a tracking device could have been placed." Eogan emptied the contents of her bag on the floor and started to sift through her personal items. He stopped when he touched a carved camel. "Where did you get this?"

"A boy at the restaurant where I met Steve sold it to me. He was insistent, and I didn't have the heart to say no."

Eogan turned it over in his hand and then twisted the head of the animal. It opened and a tiny metal device fell out. There was no mistaking what it was. It was a transmitter. Hester brought her hand up to her mouth and shook her head. That had been there the whole time she and Eogan had been trying to escape.

"They wanted you." Eogan's tone was dispassionate. "I should have checked your backpack at the airport. It is my fault that we are in this situation."

"How can it be your responsibility? I'm the one carrying a bloody tracking device in my bag." Hester shook her head. "I can't believe that sweet child was part of this. What can they possibly want with me?"

"They saw you with Steve." Eogan threw the transmitter against the wall. "Steve's purpose in this country must be suspect. They think that you are involved with his plots."

"Steve only talked about Gobekli Tepe. He knew how eager I was to see it. The only other strange behavior was when we were driving toward it and how they kept stopping and inspecting the roadside."

Panic was rising in Hester's throat. How had a simple excursion to a ruin turned into a plot from a spy movie? She put her head in her hands and tried to steady her breathing. She needed to concentrate if there was any hope of getting out of this situation alive. Now that she had found Eogan, she was determined to stay alive.

"They will not let you live."

Chapter 13

Hester jerked her head up at his words. "How did you know what I was thinking?"

"I am bonding with you." Eogan was just as surprised as Hester that he'd heard her thoughts so clearly. He had spent most of his life unable to communicate with other Hunters because of the seclusion he was kept in, and now he was not only mind connecting with Ardal, but hearing Hester's thoughts.

"What does bonding have to do with spying on someone's innermost secrets?" Her eyes narrowed.

"The bond allows us to share our feelings, emotions, and communicate without words."

"You're telepathic." Her voice rose. "Can you hear everything I think?"

"Only if you wish." Eogan sensed her outrage. "I would never invade your privacy."

Hester shoulder's sagged as if her energy had suddenly been drained from her. "I'm sorry. I'm just overwrought. Too much is happening that I don't understand."

"My only desire is to keep you safe."

"I know I sound ungrateful." She clasped her hands together. "I'm not. You could have sailed away to freedom. Instead, you insisted they take you with them. Thank you."

"I would never abandon you." She needed his help. She was incapable of fighting these men alone. "When they come for us, I will overtake them and we will break away then."

"Is that wise?" Hester's voice was full of doubt. "They have large missile-looking weapons attached to the boat, and every man is carrying an automatic machine gun. These guys mean business."

A fully armed vessel to capture one woman was unusual. If it were a coast guard patrol ship he could understand, but the craft that had stopped them hadn't announced itself. They had sped toward them and pulled in front so that the captain had no choice but to stop. He barely had enough time to warn Hester to hide before they were boarded.

Eogan stood. "It makes no sense. You must have been involved in something serious. Were these men you agreed to go to Gobekli Tepe with smugglers or spies?"

"Steve is actually Dr. Steve Jackson, an archaeologist just like me." She hesitated. "Well, he used to be. He had a good reputation until he started insisting that extraterrestrials had visited Earth in the past. He lost his teaching position and most people ignore his theories now."

"Why did you risk meeting him?" Eogan felt along the surface of the walls. There were no cracks or exposed screws that he could use as a weapon. "Your reputation could be ruined because you have associated with him."

"That's why I traveled in secrecy."

"You must have left a note or mailed someone a postcard from Turkey."

"Not even my parents."

"That means there will be no outcry when you go missing."

Hester inhaled a quick breath. "My mother and father won't have a clue where I went."

An overwhelming sensation of disbelief and horror filled Eogan as he experienced Hester's emotions. It took him a few seconds to refocus on a strategy to free her. His first concern was to calm Hester.

"I will make certain that you are able to see your parents again."

Her eyes brimmed with tears. Eogan crouched down beside her and wiped a tear from her cheek. He ached to hold her and ease her fears. It was too soon though. Hester had to accept the bond between them first. He would never violate her trust.

"They will not hurt you. You have my word as a Hunter and warrior."

The engine noise cut out and then the boat drifted. A few seconds later, it rocked against an obstacle and stopped. Hester inhaled a deep breath. "I think we're about to find out who wants me."

Eogan stood and readied himself for battle.

There was no way he was going to let these men harm Hester. He was going to get her out of this predicament. He clenched his hands into fists and waited until the door opened. Colonel Schneider appeared in the opening with a pistol directed at them. Five other men were behind him, each with machine guns aimed and ready to shoot.

"Kill the girl if he moves," Schneider snarled.

Patience was a skill Eogan had learned long ago.

He would wait for the perfect moment before killing the man.

"Walk." Schneider motioned with his gun for them to leave the room.

Eogan reached for Hester's arm and helped her stand. She was shaking and deep inside a fury burned within him. By Cygnus and Warrior she should never have to be put through this ordeal. It was against all of the laws he lived by.

He should have checked her bag. It was an error that he would not have made under normal circumstances. After finding the implant in his wrist he'd made the assumption that was how they were tracking them. Because he had been lax, Hester was in a threatening situation.

It was a mistake that he wouldn't make again.

It was obvious that Hester was involved in something serious. She might not know what her fellow explorers were really doing in Gobekli Tepe, but he was certain it hadn't been about anything as mundane as archaeology. If nothing else happened after this, he was going to track down Steve and Franklin and make them pay for the pain and fear that they had allowed Hester to be exposed to.

They were ushered off the vessel. Hester had been right about the number of guns attached to the boat. It was a military ship without a flag flying and no identifying marks on it. Eogan glanced at the weapons aimed at them. They were recent models and expensive. If a country wasn't behind their abduction, there was only one other explanation.

Albirsion Corporation.

It was the worldwide conglomerate that fronted the Albireons.

The organization was the tactical, financial, and security arm of the Albireons. It was the face that they presented to the rest of the world. They hid behind a corporate façade, which enabled them to make purchases, and takeover companies, without impunity. They made their appropriation of the world's resources, technology, and communications seem mundane. Gradually, over time, they'd put themselves in a position to conqueror the planet.

He needed to inform Ardal of what had happened. He sent out a mind connect. "*We are captured and being held by Albirsion Corporation. I will let you know the details of where we are taken.*"

"*Will you be able to escape?*"

"*Not immediately.*"

"*My team is still too far away to help.*"

"Understood."

Eogan broke the communication with Ardal, and focused on where the ship had docked. He wasn't familiar with the harbor. Once they were on land, they were pushed into the back of a military vehicle with bars and locks on the sides. These men were prepared to thwart an escape attempt. There was no way for him to break through these barriers. He would have to wait until they were in an open area or being transferred.

"Where do you think they are taking us?" Hester's voice caught in her throat.

Eogan shook his head. "I am not familiar with this place."

"Neither am I." Hester leaned against the side of the van. "It looks like we are still in Turkey though."

"There are two military bases in this country."

Eogan spoke in a calm voice. Hester was upset and he didn't want to make it worse. She didn't need to know that they were most likely being transported to Incirlik Air Base where the Albireons had access to the lower levels. They operated here without repercussions from the world's governments.

"You think these are military people?" Hester scrunched her nose. "They aren't wearing a flag on their uniform."

She was smart. "They work for the Albireons."

"All these men are traitors to the human race?" Shock and disbelief showed on her face.

"They don't know who employs them." Eogan kept his voice low. "They think they are employed by a corporation who pays well. The fact that they have the freedom to enter a military base without repercussions only validates that they are doing something that is sanctioned by their government. They have no reason to question who their employers are."

"You think they're just trying to support their family?" Hester shook her head. "They must have an idea that some of the things they do are wrong."

"Perhaps." He was not going to fault a person for protecting his loved ones. "I have no opinion why they do it. All I know is that if they harm you, they will die."

"What good will that do if I'm dead?" Hester shut her eyes for a second. "It all seems so hopeless."

"We will escape." Eogan's voice was forceful. "You will live."

"I was a fool." Self-recrimination was evident in her voice. "I trusted a man I had only met on the internet."

"You knew his reputation."

"True, but that wasn't enough." Hester straightened her shoulders. "There's no point in regrets. How are we going to escape?"

"When we reach the facility I will assess its weaknesses. Once I know their intentions, then I will act."

"So basically we need to keep our eyes open for an opportunity."

"Yes."

"What if one doesn't appear?"

"I will make it happen. I won't do anything until I know you'll be safe." Eogan sensed that panic was rising within Hester. He sent her a wave of calm. She had to be focused and strong for what lay ahead. Breaking out of a military compound was not an easy task and he couldn't afford to have her terror impede their escape. "You need to stay composed if this is going to work."

She nodded and took a deep breath. "I'll do my best."

"Think of it like an archaeological ruin."

"You want me to look for clues about its purpose, and the reasoning of the people who built it?" Hester's voice was doubtful.

"If you understand the builders, then you should be able to find an escape route."

Eogan watched Hester's reaction to his words. She was an intelligent woman and her perspective was different than his. If they were going to where he suspected, then it would be almost impossible to break free. That wasn't an option. Hester must live at all costs.

He had never been unsuccessful in a mission. It would take luck and timing to elude guards and all the barriers to their release. If he had to decimate the base and all its occupants to ensure Hester's liberty, he would do it.

He would not fail this time.

The van stopped and the slamming of doors vibrated through the enclosed space. It was time to begin planning their escape. Eogan hoped that there would be an opportunity now before they were led below ground. Once they were inside it would be more difficult to gain freedom.

"Ready?"

Hester nodded. "I'll look at this place with the eyes of an archaeologist."

The doors opened and the lock holding the bars of their cage was removed. There were three men pointing machine guns at them. One of them motioned with his weapon for them to step out. Eogan let Hester precede him. Once he was on the outside, he stood in front of her. He would block any bullets coming her way.

His eyes narrowed as he took in their surroundings. He hadn't been mistaken. They were at a military base. Wire fence and guard posts surrounded them on all sides. In the distance was an airstrip that was lined with F-16 fighter jets. Their immediate vicinity was devoid of people, vehicles, and buildings. Beyond the gates and fencing was a barren landscape. It was impossible to evaluate what resources they would have access to when they were free.

It also meant that they would make easy targets once they were beyond the gates.

They were pushed into a four-story high metal building that looked like a hangar from the outside. Inside it was a different story. This wasn't part of the regular military base. Everywhere there were concrete barriers with men standing guard. Laser sights were trained on their chests and heads. One wrong move and they would be shot instantly. They were marched past the soldiers and stopped at a large bank of elevators.

Eogan could feel Hester's anxiety rising.

He sent her a wave of calm.

He was familiar with the type of structure that they were in. It was very similar to the one at Pine Gap. That would make it easier to execute an escape. The Albireons would be on the lower levels. They would never risk humans seeing their true form. Secrecy and lies were the weapons they used against the species that they mined for genes.

The holding cells were also below ground.

It would be difficult, but not impossible to escape. There were always opportunities when the doors were open or when someone came in to interrogate. It might seem insurmountable to Hester, but to a Hunter, skilled and trained in the improbable and unforeseen, it would prove easy enough.

He felt her tremble beside him. He pulled her close and let her lean her head on his shoulder. A wave of peace and purpose flowed through him. He knew that at all costs, she must not be hurt. All his years of training had led to this point. As incredible a task as it seemed to break out of this secure area, he was going to do it.

There was one major issue with a structure like this.

Mind connection with other Hunters was blocked.

While one of the guards pushed the elevator button, Eogan sent out another message to Ardal. *"We are at Incirlik Air Base. It is similar to Pine Gap so I will not be able to communicate."*

"Where exactly are you in the base?"

"We are in the northwest hangar. It is underground and the Albireons will be at the lower levels."

"I will alert the team to your location."

The door opened and they were moved inside. Hester inhaled a sharp breath and Eogan tightened his grip on her shoulder. He sent her as much strength and reassurance as possible. The quiet life of a university professor was no preparation for the battle they had in front of them. He felt her straighten her shoulders.

They stopped at the fourth floor.

They were ushered down a long narrow hallway. Eogan scanned the ceiling for the security cameras. The monitoring lens were placed at the intersection of halls. They continued turning down hallways until it felt as if they were in a maze. He counted the turns and memorized the route back to the lift. When they reached the end of the last hallway, they were halted.

A door was opened.

They were pushed inside.

It took a second for Eogan's eyes to adjust to the dull light of their cell. When he did, he realized they weren't alone. Two men were standing against the far wall. One was in his fifties with a long white beard and spectacles perched on the end of his nose. The other was in his twenties, skinny, and standing with his arms crossed. His stance was one of defiance.

Their clothes were tattered and dirty. They looked as if they hadn't slept in a while and their eyes were wary. Hester was behind him, but with the slam of the steel door, she moved away.

The men's eyes widened when they saw her.

"Hester!" The older man took a step forward. "I thought they had killed you."

She rushed to the man and hugged him. "I'm glad to see you're alive. What happened?"

"We were tracked down and captured sometime last night." He shrugged. "Time is hard to judge when you can't see the daylight."

Eogan's eyes narrowed.

His patience had been rewarded.

These were the men that had abandoned Hester by the roadside. They had left her defenseless and in a dangerous situation. Their actions were responsible for almost getting her killed. They were also guilty of being involved in activities that had seen to Hester being tracked and incarcerated by the Albireons.

There was only one course of action for him.

"You have endangered a woman's life." Eogan grabbed the younger man by his collar and pushed him high up the wall. "For that you must die."

Chapter 14

Hester dropped her bag and rushed over to Eogan. She tried to pull his arm away from Franklin's neck. "You can't kill him."

"They deserted you. You could have died." Eogan's grip loosened slightly. "They broke the Sacred Code."

"They didn't know what those men intended." She looked up at Franklin, noting the look of terror in his eyes. "At least I don't think they did."

"Why did you abandon Hester?" Eogan's voice reverberated throughout the small cell.

"Everything happened so fast." Steve Jackson spoke in a shaky voice. "One minute we were being blocked by a jeep and the next these armed thugs were dragging Josh and Hester away from the vehicle. Franklin saw his break and he took it."

"You did not come back to help." Eogan's voice held disdain. "That is the action of a coward."

The taunt seemed to motivate Franklin into action. He pulled on Eogan's hands and bucked his body in an effort to escape. It was futile. Hester knew that Eogan wouldn't let the man down until he had the answers he needed.

"Please just tell him why you ran." Hester's voice was more of a plea than an order.

"How do I know I can trust him?" Franklin's mouth twisted into a sneer. "He's just some guy you picked up along the way."

How dare he suggest that she was in the habit of picking up strangers in foreign countries?

Hester sensed the cold determination building in Eogan. She should defuse the situation, but after Franklin's last remark, she no longer cared what happened to him. Instead of helping her, he'd been concerned with saving his own skin. Eogan was right.

Franklin was a coward.

Indignation and fury burned inside of her.

"You were a stranger and look where that got me." Hester didn't hide her contempt. "Since I met you, I've been shot at, nearly raped, watched men die, kidnapped, bugged, and thrown into a cell with you. I did, however, get to see Gobekli Tepe."

She turned away and walked to the far corner. Anger was clouding her judgement and she needed a few minutes to calm down. All the testosterone in the room was making that impossible. She crossed her arms and sat with her back against the wall, her legs stretched out in front of her. She shut her eyes and leaned her head against the cool stone of the prison cell.

"You have upset her."

Eogan's voice had a soothing effect on her. The only good thing about this crazy situation was that he was still with her. She didn't know how she would have survived this ordeal without his strength and support. She sighed and opened her eyes. Nothing had changed. Eogan was still holding Franklin high against the wall.

"Let me go." Franklin twisted his body from side to side.

"We didn't mean for Hester to be hurt." Steve's voice was a calm in the middle of the storm. "It was important that we get away from those men."

"Why go there in the first place?" Eogan asked.

"We had an assignation with another contact." Steve's voice was apologetic. "I should have insisted that Hester stay in the city, but I didn't see any harm in bringing her along."

"Who was this person?"

"Don't tell him," Franklin shouted as he frantically increased his struggle to break Eogan's hold.

"We're all in here together. That means we have to trust each other." Steve was the voice of reason.

"Enough." Hester was tired of listening to their arguing. "Put him down Eogan." She jabbed a finger at Steve and then Franklin. "You two had better start talking. Why was a transmitter hidden in my bag, and who were you going to meet?"

Eogan released Franklin.

The man fell to the ground with a thud.

Hester hid her smile. Eogan turned to her and she saw a twinkle in his eye. He'd done it on purpose and she couldn't fault him. It served Franklin right. A little embarrassment was a small price after everything she'd been through in the past twenty-four hours.

"That was uncalled for." Steve put a hand under Franklin's arm and helped him stand. "This man is trying to save humanity. He deserves better treatment."

Eogan was walking toward her.

He stopped at Steve's words.

"How is he going to do that?" Eogan's voice held mild curiosity.

Hester couldn't see Franklin saving the world unless it was with a peaceful demonstration. He certainly didn't look to be someone who could do battle. Look at how he'd behaved when they'd been stopped outside Gobekli Tepe. He and Steve had run away at the first sign of trouble.

"He's a leader in the H.R.F." Steve voice held a note of awe.

Eogan crossed his arms and glared at the two men. "Explain."

"We don't have to tell you anything." Franklin brushed his pants off. "You're nothing but a bully. People like you are why the world is at risk."

"Humans were in trouble long before I crashed on this planet."

Eogan's words hung in the air for a few seconds before Steve cleared his throat. "Did you say crashed?"

Hester's protective instincts kicked in. She knew Steve was concerned about aliens being on Earth because of their past conversations. She was less certain of Franklin, and she didn't trust him. Eogan was capable of defending himself, but she didn't want this to escalate to a fight before she found out about this supposed organization that Franklin was involved in.

She stood and went to Eogan's side. "Explain what H.R.F. means. That's the least you can do after abandoning me."

"I don't owe you anything." Franklin straightened his shoulders. "You're just another one of those silly people who think that every alien that comes to Earth is a friend. Now you might find out what is really happening on this planet."

"You will speak to her with respect or I will not be responsible for what happens to you."

Franklin put his hands on his hips. "What is with you and this protection stuff?"

"Women are to be obeyed."

"Where the hell did you come up with that?" Franklin shook his head. "Every word from your mouth is crazy. Where did you pick this guy up?"

"The Sacred Code is what I follow and Hester did not pick me up. I found her being attacked, and helped."

"How?" Franklin snorted. "Did you talk them to death with your craziness?"

"I killed them."

Steve raised his eyebrows and looked at her for confirmation. "They shot Josh and the others. I was seconds away from being raped when Eogan stepped in and took care of the men."

"And you wonder why you're in this place?" Franklin shook his head. "How can you possibly stay with a lunatic?"

"I insisted." Eogan crossed his arms. "When they boarded the ship we were on, I knew they meant her harm. When the time is right I will kill them too."

Steve pushed his glasses up his nose. "Is this true?"

Hester nodded. "He's very good at killing."

"Did you escape from an institution for the criminally insane?" Franklin moved back.

"I have been trained since birth to be a warrior. I uphold the Sacred Code and the punishment for disobeying is death."

Steve who had been watching Eogan closely took a step toward him.

"I've read something like that before." Steve's voice rose in excitement. "It was when I was doing researching on the internet."

Eogan stared down at him. "Reading is not going to help you in this situation."

Steve shook his head. "You misunderstand. I remember an organization of men who hired their services out. They said the exact same thing. They had been trained since birth to be warriors. They called themselves Hunters."

Eogan didn't say anything. Hester reached an arm out to him. "Is it possible that this group is similar to you?"

Eogan nodded. "They are the ones I seek. I have been in communication with their leader, Ardal."

Steve took a step back. "You're a Hunter?"

"Yes."

"Help us escape." Franklin seemed to forget his earlier aversion and moved closer to Eogan. "We'll pay you."

"Hunters have been bred and trained to be the best warriors in the universe. I fight with honor."

"We're a good cause. Steve and I were trying to join the H.R.F. and that's how we got captured."

"What is the H.R.F.?" Hester was tired of hearing the letters without knowing what they stood for.

"It's the Human Resistance Force." Steve spoke in a solemn voice. "What most of the world doesn't know is that there are aliens who are controlling our planet and killing humans."

She frowned. "So this is a group who is trying to kill these extraterrestrials?"

"It is crazy to attack them." Eogan crossed his arms. "They have strength in too many places for any siege to be effective."

"What do you know about this?" Franklin scoffed. "One minute you are upholding some code by killing people, and the next, you think you know about aliens."

"I know the Albireons intimately." Eogan's voice was low. "I have been held captive by them for over thirty years. I know what their weaknesses are and where they are hiding."

Franklin's eyes widened. "How come you're still alive?"

"I was controlled by humans who worked with the Albireons. I was sent on many missions to kill. I have no love for their race or the people who work with them."

A renewed appreciated for what Eogan had suffered welled up within Hester. It was as if it had happened to her. She was overwhelmed by the despair and isolation of his situation. It was atrocious that Eogan had been used as a weapon by those monsters. They'd exploited him because in their eyes, he was less than human. He was an alien without emotions or feeling. It was wrong.

Anger and outrage filled her.

Those men deserved to die.

"I will kill them when the time is right." Eogan's voice echoed in her head.

She felt a whisper of a connection in her mind and knew that it was Eogan reaching out to her. He'd heard and sensed her thoughts. It was an intimate awareness. One of attraction and belonging, and she delighted in knowing that it was only between the two of them.

She turned to Steve. "Were you planning on meeting with this group while you were with me?"

"I meant to tell you about them, but there was no time."

"How did they find out about your plans?"

Steve gave her a sheepish look. "I don't think I believed there were really aliens controlling humans. I wasn't as careful with my communications as I should have been."

Everything was now clear. She'd been communicating with Steve on the internet for months. They had discussed the possibility of extraterrestrials being on the planet in the past and the present. If he'd told her about a movement to rid the world of these beings, then she would probably have agreed to join.

She looked at Franklin. "What is your connection? The trouble didn't begin until you joined us on our trip to Gobekli Tepe."

"I made contact with someone in the H.R.F. and they were going to meet us at the site."

"So it was a trap and you lied about being a leader in their organization." Eogan shook his head. "You should have scouted the ruins before going there. I doubt there was ever a legitimate meeting."

"You're wrong." Franklin's face reddened. "I made certain."

"Were you introduced in person or was it an internet communication?"

Franklin opened his mouth to speak and then shut it. He glanced down at the floor and then shrugged. "They seemed to be real."

"Does the organization exist?" Hester had to know.

"Yes." Steve cleared his throat. "I found mention of them, but it wasn't through regular channels. They are very secretive and elusive."

"They would have to be. The Albireon reach is far. Few live to talk about them."

"So what does that mean for us?" Franklin whined.

"It means they will kill you. First, they will demand information about this H.R.F. organization."

"We don't know anything." Franklin's voice rose hysterically. "There's nothing to find out."

"They will make certain that you have no knowledge before they end your life."

"Great." Franklin rolled his eyes. "Are you trying to scare us? It won't work. We've been sitting in this cell for hours and have had plenty of time to prepare ourselves."

"They will use torture. Only your death will assure them that you are telling the truth. The methods on this planet are primitive." Eogan spoke matter of fact. "Do you know how to withstand pain?"

Steve's eyes widened and he shook his head. "Surely it won't come to that. We have rights."

"These people work outside of the laws of any country."

A shiver went through Hester. They had tracked her because they thought she was involved with the H.R.F. Pain was not something she was comfortable with. She hated needles. Going to the dentist sent her into a panic attack. She doubted she'd ever be able to withstand torture, especially when she didn't know anything.

"It will not come to that." Eogan turned to her. His eyes were intense and sincere. "I will make certain you are safe no matter what."

Hester blinked to stop the tears that threatened to overcome her. Eogan would risk everything to shield her. He had already proven that. To have a man protect her at all costs was more than she had ever hoped for. She had envisioned her years ahead as a lonely spinster who had her research and teaching to keep her occupied.

In that moment she knew the truth.

She loved him.

Hester gave him a tremulous smile and leaned her head against his chest. "Thank you."

There was a loud banging outside the cell and before she could react, Eogan turned to the door and stood in front of her. When she tried to move, his arm blocked her. She heard the door open, but all she could see was Eogan's back.

"There's no point in hiding her." A man's gruff voice filled the air. "You and the woman are to follow us. Schneider has some questions."

Chapter 15

Every muscle in Eogan's body tightened as he prepared for battle. Hester's fear was palpable. She had to know that he would not let these men harm her in any way. The connection between them was growing, and he knew deep within his being that she was his pair bond. He would die protecting her, but his death meant nothing if she was still a prisoner.

Hester's safety had to be ensured before he attacked.

That required timing and patience.

He would act only when he knew that he could free her from this prison. Their jailers thought they had the upper hand. They didn't realize they were dealing with a Hunter and that gave him an advantage. One he would use when the time was right.

The man motioned them to the door.

Eogan's hand curled around Hester's waist and he brought her close so he could shield her with his body. She was precious to him. He would guarantee her survival. He sent a wave of comfort and squeezed her arm in reassurance. In a few seconds he felt her relax.

"Move." The lead man ordered. He pointed his weapon at the door before turning to their companions. "You two stay here."

Eogan's tension eased. His only concern was Hester. If he survived, he would consider coming back for the others, but only if she insisted. They had abandoned her to die. They had no honor. There was no value in saving such men.

Hester's breathing rate increased as they left the cell and were steered down a narrow passage. Eogan did his best to send her comfort. Until she was outside of this underground structure, real peace wasn't possible for either of them. Instead, he kept sending her a mind connection. *Soon you will be free.* He wasn't sure if she could hear him, but her body eased beside him.

They were led into an interrogation room with a table and four chairs.

"Sit. Colonel Schneider will be in to talk with you."

When they were seated she leaned toward him. "Do you think

they'll let us go?"

"No." Lying to Hester wasn't a possibility. "I am ready for battle."

"Is that wise?" There was a quiver in her voice.

"It is necessary." Eogan reached for her hand. "These men are ruthless. They have much blood on their conscience. I will not let them have yours."

A tremor went through Hester. "Promise you will stay safe. I couldn't continue if something happened to you."

Eogan lowered his voice. "A Hunter's bond is present even in death."

"I need a live man." Hester's tone was strident. "A voice in my head does not replace years of loneliness."

Eogan's heart lightened. She sounded irritated. It was a sign she was getting tougher, and she needed strength for the fight ahead.

"Is that an order?" he asked.

"You bet." Hester leaned back in her chair. "I'm not the only one walking out of here alive."

"It is my greatest wish to do your bidding." Eogan heard a disturbance in the hall and inclined his head in that direction. "Take cover when I start."

Hester straightened her shoulders. "Just give me the word."

No further conversation was possible. The door opened, and Colonel Schneider walked in accompanied by three armed guards. Eogan eyed up their weapons and assessed what was necessary to overpower them. It should be easy. The man closest to him was holding his gun with a light grip. Once he had taken him out, the rest would fall.

"I'm glad to see you two are getting comfortable." The colonel threw papers on the table. "You've left a wake of dead bodies behind you."

"You've fabricated that." Hester put her elbows on the table. "I'm not strong enough to kill anyone."

"Maybe not you Dr. Adams, but your friend here is more than capable." Schneider glared at Eogan. "It's a funny thing about you. I ran your picture through our computer recognition system and it came up empty. I find it hard to believe that a man as skilled in killing as you, wouldn't be on someone's data bank."

"You must be mistaken then." Eogan clamped his lips tight. The longer they stayed in the dark about his identity, the easier it would be to escape.

"Your record will show up." The colonel opened his file folder. "Now, you're an interesting person, Dr. Adams. You're an archeologist caught up in a subversive organization."

"Your information is wrong." Hester's voice was only mildly curious. "I came to Turkey to see Gobekli Tepe."

"Strangely enough, we found a lot of dead men there." The colonel tapped his fingers on the file folder. "I doubt that is a coincidence."

She shrugged. "They attacked one of my colleagues."

"A Joshua Graves to be exact." Schneider looked up from his papers and glared at Hester. "He's a subversive known to us."

"Who are you?" Hester's tone was aggressive. "I'm an American citizen and you have no right to hold me against my will."

"Ah, but I do." The colonel raised an eyebrow. "You are in my custody and will remain so for the rest of your life. No one leaves here."

Hester sat back and crossed her arms. "Nobody has that much power."

"You and your collaborators know exactly what we're capable of." He leaned forward. "It was foolish to rebel against us. Now, I need the names of your contacts."

"I wouldn't give you information like that even if I knew."

Schneider chuckled. "That's where you're wrong. Once I send you a few more floors below ground, we'll know everything about you. There are no defenses against the techniques our friends use."

Hester frowned. "Is this another secret government agency?"

"You know who they are." Schneider slammed his folder shut. "The Albireons have helped us for years. The threat you and your friends represent will not be tolerated. You will tell us everything you know, and after that, I will enjoy watching you die."

"Enough." Eogan growled. "I will not allow you to threaten the life of a woman and not take action."

"Try it." Schneider's moved back from the table. "No man escapes here alive."

Eogan's patience had ended.

The man was overly confident and that would be his downfall.

He pushed Hester on the ground at the same time as he elbowed the man beside him in the gut and grabbed his rifle. He aimed and killed one soldier before the others could react. Eogan stood and pulled the still groaning victim of his elbow in front of him. He used him as a shield. The two other soldiers fired their weapons, killing their comrade.

Eogan shot both of them through the forehead before turning the gun on Schneider.

"Who are you?" He was reaching for his weapon.

"I am a Hunter." He shot the colonel through the heart. "No man threatens a woman and lives."

Eogan then shot him in the forehead.

Schneider fell face forward on the table.

In the next second, the door to the room opened and three other military men barged in firing their weapons.

Eogan continued to use the lifeless soldier in his arms as a shield and killed the new arrivals. There was silence after that. He steadied his breathing as he waited and listened for reinforcements. None came. Eogan dropped the dead man, and went to the door. He checked the hallway for more attackers, but it was empty. Schneider had underestimated his enemy. It was a serious mistake that had proved fatal for the colonel.

Eogan reentered the interrogation room and shut the door.

Hester was still on the floor, shielded by the table.

She looked up at him. "Are you hurt?" Her voice was shaking.

Eogan shook his head. "We need to go. They have to report on a regular basis. One missed call will alert the base to a problem."

Hester scrambled out from under the table and grabbed her bag. "I'm more than ready to leave this place."

"Stay behind me."

Eogan swung the strap of the rifle over his shoulder and picked up two abandoned pistols. He put one in his waistband, and kept the other in his hand as he opened the door. He checked the hall again. It was clear. He motioned Hester to follow him. Together they left the room and started down the maze of hallways. If this place was like Pine Gap, the bank of elevators would be in the center. He moved in that direction.

Footsteps sounded from one of the corridors.

Eogan flattened his side against the wall, keeping Hester covered.

He felt her hands flutter against his back, and as much as he longed to take her in his arms and comfort her, he forced himself to focus on whoever was headed their direction. Within seconds, the men had rounded the corner. There were three in all.

Eogan grabbed the first one by the neck and used his weapon to shoot the next two before tightening his hold on his captive. "Report that everything is okay."

He snatched the man's radio and jerked him tighter before holding it to his mouth. "Now."

"Everything is under control," the soldier said.

Eogan turned the transmitter off.

He then pulled the entry card from his prisoner's waistband and handed it to Hester. "Unlock the door across the way."

Once it was open, he hauled his prisoner into it and hit him over the head with the end of the pistol. The man dropped to the ground unconscious. Eogan dragged the two dead men into the room, and then locked the door. He picked up their assault rifles from the hall floor, and slung them on his shoulder. He would need all the firing power at his disposal to get them out of the base.

"That should give us extra time."

Hester nodded, but Eogan could tell she was shaken by what had happened. He pulled her close. "There was no choice. It might have been more merciful if I'd killed the last man because once the Albireons find out he failed, they will order him shot."

"It's all so horrible." Hester's voice was hoarse. "Yesterday I didn't know that such a place like this existed. Now, I'll never forget it."

"We can worry about this once we're off the base." Eogan took her hand and started down the hall. "I will not rest until I know you are safe."

They reached the bank of elevators, and when the door opened, Eogan stretched up and hit the camera with the butt of one of the assault weapons. They would send someone to check the malfunctioning unit, but they would have already made their escape from the base. He took the entry card from Hester and swiped it before pushing the ground button. The elevator jerked and then began its ascent.

Hester opened her mouth to speak, but he pressed a finger against her lips. They may not see them, but the audio feed would still be connected. She seemed to understand right away and instead of speaking, she leaned into him. He sent her strength and energy.

There was still a long way to go before they would be free. The elevator stopped with a jerk on the second floor. Eogan pulled Hester behind him and moved to the side, gun ready to shoot. He eased the tension from his muscles and waited.

"I hope you can convince him we need a reasonable solution to this problem." A male voice was speaking just outside the open door. Eogan could see the man's reflection in the shiny metal on the rear elevator wall. The man was alone, and he was holding something in his hand.

His chest tightened as he recognized the voice.

It was General Carter, his handler from Pine Gap.

"I'm all for using force in this situation." The general paused for a few seconds and then the sound of the elevator bell had him turning toward the open door. "I don't know who they've captured, but Schneider thinks I should handle it personally."

Eogan stilled his breathing.

Fear was emanating from Hester, but he blocked it. His complete focus on this situation was necessary if they were to stay alive. Every cell in his body screamed to kill this man who had caused him so much pain over the years. He had to hold himself back from jumping out of the elevator and ripping his enemy apart with his bare hands.

Hester was the reason he hesitated.

He couldn't risk endangering her life.

The general had to finish his telephone conversation before he could kill him. Anything else was too risky and might alert someone to their escape. Once he hung up, then Eogan would attack.

"I think we need to handle this before it gets out of control. There are too many eyes on it." The general put his hand on the elevator door to prevent it shutting. "Let me assess the prisoner on Level Four and see what she knows. I'll get back to you."

They had just escaped from Level Four.

Hester was the situation that needed to be handled. If Carter was involved, then that meant certain death. He didn't care about gathering information. He had authorized the ambush to kill Eogan and the other members of the raiding team in Syria. Once a person was of no further use, Carter had them eliminated. He would do the same with Hester.

There was only one solution.

Carter had to die.

As the man took a step toward the elevator, Eogan readied

himself.

Chapter 16

Hester's worst fears had come true.

Within seconds, they would be captured again.

Hester held her breath and shut her eyes. She willed the man to move away from the elevator. She'd seen too much death in the last few minutes, and she didn't think she could stomach anymore. Eogan would kill this man. She had no doubt of that. It was only a matter of timing.

A phone rang.

The man took his hand off the door and answered. "Carter here."

The door closed, and the elevator continued its ascent. Hester released the breath she'd been holding and leaned her head against Eogan's back. That had been close. She didn't know if she was up to any more of this adventure. She might have longed for excitement when she was huddled in her cozy apartment doing research, but she'd had enough.

Adventure was overrated.

There was a lot to be said for living a boring life.

A second later, the doors opened, and they walked out into a huge structure. She looked around the hangar-like building, noting the parked military vehicles and the sounds of music coming from somewhere on the right. She'd been wrong with her first assessment. The place wasn't empty, she just couldn't see anyone.

"That was General Carter." Eogan's low voice rumbled through her.

"You knew him?"

Eogan nodded. "He was my handler for many years. He sent me on my last mission. It was an ambush and intended to kill me."

"It's a good thing we got out of that interrogation room when we did." Hester shivered as she considered what could have happened if Eogan had been found out.

"We do not have long before they send someone after us."

Eogan motioned her to a delivery truck ten feet away. The logo on the side announced that it was an international courier service and its rear door was open. Maybe she could mail herself home?

Hester moved fast to keep pace with Eogan who was heading for the vehicle. When he got there, he looked underneath and then inside. The driver was nowhere in sight. Eogan grabbed her by the waist and hoisted her up into the truck. He crouched low, and she saw him move to the side and examine the wheels. A minute later he was back.

"They checked the truck going into the base." Eogan jumped up beside her. "There will be no need to check it when it leaves."

"Are you certain?" Hester looked around at the packages piled high against the steel panel walls.

"No, but we'll take that chance." Eogan moved her behind a large box. "To be safe, you will hide."

"What about you?"

"I need to insure the driver doesn't deviate from his route. If he does, then I will take over the driving."

"That means you'll kill him."

"Only if he's a threat." Eogan would have said more but the stomping of boots stopped him.

He moved closer and crouched down beside her. He was like a beautiful animal of prey, his body poised to attack at the slightest provocation. Hester marveled that they had made it this far. There were voices and footsteps approaching them. She held her breath and strained her ears to listen to what was being said outside of the truck. Snippets of words were all that came through.

Delivery.

Speed.

Next time.

There was a scraping sound at the rear door and then the thump of something being thrown into the vehicle. Seconds became minutes as Hester listened to boxes being loaded. As long as they kept the packages near the door, and didn't reorganize the load, they should be safe. Several beats of silence were followed by the slam of metal against metal when the rear door was shut.

She exhaled the breath she'd been holding and sagged against a box behind her. She heard the cab door of the truck open and then the engine roar to life. They moved ahead with a jolt and the sound of grinding gears. Hester's heartbeat returned to normal. They had made it past the first barrier to freedom.

Hester plopped down on the floor. Her legs were too weak to

hold her up any longer. If they had to run again she needed to conserve her strength. Eogan, didn't seem to tire. She felt a glow of heat race through her as she thought about his declaration. They were pair bonds. She didn't care what he called it.

It was love.

Love had entered her life after she'd given up all hope of ever finding it. She wanted to hold it tight and luxuriate in the bliss and euphoria that surrounded her whole being. She was in love and it was heavenly.

Eogan glanced over at her. "You are happy." It was a statement, not a question.

She nodded. He'd sensed her feelings. "When will we know we're safe?"

"The driver has to pass two gates before he will be on the outside. There should be a quick inspection of his logbook and then they'll let him through."

"I hope so." Hester sighed. "I want to go home."

"We will arrange that after we are free. There will be no tracking device this time." Eogan's voice was a low whisper as the truck geared down. "This is the first checkpoint."

Hester ducked further behind the box and Eogan moved to the opposite side of the van. If someone looked in from the rear, they wouldn't be able to see either of them. The voice of the driver was a mumble of words she couldn't interpret. She clenched her fingers together and waited to see if they passed the barrier.

Seconds later, the truck was in motion again.

She grinned over at Eogan. "One more guard post."

Eogan nodded, and loosened his hold on the assault rifle. He checked the magazine for cartridges and then reinserted it into the gun. Hester's eyes widened. He was preparing for a confrontation. It had to be a precaution. They'd made it through the first barrier without a problem.

The next stop was several minutes later. Again, she snuggled further into the boxes. Eogan did the same, with one exception, he aimed the rifle at the door. She heard the distinct sound of boots walking along the side of the truck.

The footsteps stopped at the rear.

A bang reverberated through the metal box of the truck before the latch was pushed aside. Hester brought her arms and legs closer to her body, trying to become as small as possible. As long as they only took a look from the outside, they would be safe. Her breath caught in her throat and she closed her eyes so she wouldn't see what was happening.

She felt the rush of air on her face when the rear door opened. There were the voices of several men and what sounded like someone stepping onto the vehicle. A few more words and then the scraping sound of boxes being shoved aside. Her heart beat frantically as she waited for them to walk further into the truck. Once they did, Eogan would have no choice but to shoot.

Footsteps came toward her and stopped.

She heard the tearing of paper.

The slide of cardboard against metal boomed in her ears.

The stomp of boots echoed as someone turned and moved to the exit. They jumped down with a soft thud, and Hester eased the tension in her body. They weren't in the clear yet, but they were safe for a few minutes longer. She prayed they would let them leave and not call for someone else to search the truck.

Time dragged to a halt as she counted the seconds with her heartbeats.

A wave of calm flowed through her.

She opened her eyes and stared into the dark orbs of Eogan. She saw her future in his gaze. His gun was aimed and ready to defend them. No matter what happened at this check station, they would survive. Even if he had to kill all the guards and drive the truck himself, they would escape this place.

The men's voices were low and then she heard the slam of the rear door. They must have been satisfied with what they'd seen because the footsteps moved away. Hester exhaled a deep breath and leaned back. All they had to do was wait for the driver to pull away from the base and their escape would be complete.

They drove for several miles before the vehicle jerked to the right and slowed down.

Eogan motioned for her to join him. "He is stopping."

"Is it scheduled?"

He shook his head. "I punctured one of the front tires so it would leak air slow enough he'd make it through the base, but not into town."

"Wouldn't it have been easier for us to escape in a populated area?"

"Too dangerous."

Eogan waited until the truck stopped and then unlatched the rear door. He jumped down and held his arms up for her. Once she was on the ground, he closed the door and they rushed to the opposite side of the road. The driver was just leaving the cab of the vehicle by the time they had found cover behind some rocks.

"Can you walk?"

"I'll have to." Hester stayed low and followed Eogan until they were out of sight, then she stood and stretched. "How much time before they start the search?"

"They'll look for the truck first."

"So that's why you wanted us to leave?" She was impressed.

Eogan offered his hand so she could scramble down a shallow ditch. "We must keep moving. We have to find shelter so that we can avoid any aerial detection."

They walked for about an hour and stopped when they came to a rocky area that provided protection. Eogan found a stream and once they had drank their fill and refilled the water bottle in her bag, they moved back into the cover of the rocks. Hester sighed and sat with her back against the cool stone. It had been a long couple of days and there was still more to go before they were out of danger.

Eogan was standing guard at the opening of the short cavern they were resting in. His eyes never left the horizon as he scanned the ground and then the sky. He was an expert in the military aspects of this operation, and she was thankful he was with her. She wouldn't have survived on her own.

"What about Steve and Franklin?" Her thoughts went to the two men who were still prisoners at the base. "Shouldn't we rescue them?"

"It cannot be done." He turned to her.

"Nothing is impossible." Hester didn't want to think about the fate that awaited the men. Schneider had been adamant. He didn't care what he did to get the truth. "They'll be killed if we don't try."

"They left you to die." Eogan crouched down beside her. "They have no honor."

"True, but that doesn't mean their lives aren't worth saving." Hester wiped a strand of hair from her face. "Steve is a very nice man."

"Nice does not protect you. These people will not believe that he had no knowledge of this H.R.F. group they are looking for."

She shrugged. "I've never heard of them before. Have you?"

"They were not one of my targets."

"If they were, they would be dead." Hester finished the words she was certain Eogan was about to say.

"Yes."

"I think I'm sensing your thoughts," Hester said. "How does that work?"

"I have only heard the legends about pair bonds and the connection between them. Hunters can mind connect from birth. Places below ground and with electronic blocking mechanisms, like Pine Gap where I was stationed, can block those connections."

It took Hester a second to realize the significance of what he had said. "You guys communicate with your thoughts?"

Eogan nodded. "I have been in contact with the leader of the Hunter unit on Earth. He is aware that we have escaped from the base."

"Does that mean they will help us?" A glimmer of hope lightened the tension in her chest.

"They are too far away." Eogan gave her a searching look. "You look exhausted. Sleep and I will keep watch. We still have a long distance to go."

"You haven't slept either."

"I am a warrior. I am trained for this."

Hester didn't have the energy to arguing with him. He was right. She was tired and surviving on pure adrenaline. A rest was what she needed and even the hard surface of this rocky area looked like heaven. She punched her bag into a pillow and put her head down. Sleep came fast and deep.

She didn't move until she felt the shaking of her shoulder.

She opened her eyes to darkness.

Eogan was leaning over her. "There is someone approaching. Can you stand?"

Hester nodded. "Are they from the base?"

"They came in the opposite direction." He helped her to her feet. "I wanted to be certain you were awake before I captured them."

"Thanks." She was on full alert now. "Try not to kill them until you find out if they are after us."

"There would be no honor in killing an innocent person."

Eogan edged along the rocky wall. She watched him disappear around the opening. Fear skittered up her spine. What if there were too many of them for Eogan to handle? He was important to her, and the last thing she wanted was to lose him.

Hester picked up her bag. If he needed aid, then she would give it. She'd had enough of letting things happen to her. It was time she took a stand and helped. She might not be able to kill someone, but she could distract them. She wasn't going to continue living life on the sidelines.

Hester was about to step into the open, when the sound of a scuffle halted her. Eogan had found the intruders. In the dim light of the setting sun, she saw him grab one person by the arm and aim his gun at two others standing in front of him. Their arms were in the air. They had no apparent weapons and weren't resisting Eogan.

"What are you doing here?" Eogan's voice was a low hiss.

"Don't hurt us." A man's voice pleaded. "We've come from the H.R.F."

Chapter 17

Eogan recognized one of the men standing in front of him.

It was Captain Barton.

The same man that had led the mission into an ambush in Syria. He had assumed the man had died with the rest of the team. He had been wrong. It was dangerous to make a mistake like that and this might be the time to correct it. He threw the man he was holding to the ground and aimed his weapon at the captain.

"Why should I believe you?" Eogan pulled back the trigger of his pistol. "You were on the mission that was intended to kill me."

"It was meant to destroy all of us." Barton's hands stayed high in the air. "We just want to talk."

"About what?"

"How you escaped from Incirlik?"

At that moment, Hester came out of the rock shelter. "It can't hurt if you hear them out."

Eogan pointed to Captain Barton. "This man was on the raid with me that was ambushed. He is Albirsion Corporation Security."

"Not anymore." Captain Barton motioned to the stone overhang. "It would be better if we didn't discuss this in the open."

Eogan looked up. So far there had been no drones sent out to search for them, but that didn't mean there weren't satellites combing the area from space. They were safer out of sight or moving. He waved his gun at the men, motioning them to go before him. He pushed Hester behind him and followed.

It wasn't much of a shelter. The rock blocked them from any surveillance and that was all that mattered. When they were inside, Hester pulled her flashlight from her bag, and flicked it on before setting it on its end. The beam of light provided an eerie, surreal atmosphere. It also let Eogan assess each of the men that he held captive.

Captain Barton was in charge. He was still in his military uniform which was tattered and torn. There were stains, probably blood, on his sleeves and the insignia of the Albirsion Corporation had been ripped off.

Next to him, was a slim man with a scrawny mustache and narrow nose. He wore a dark woolen cap and black camouflage paint on his face. He looked too young to be allowed outside this late at night.

The other man was older. He had alert eyes that followed every movement Eogan made. This man had seen battle even though he wasn't in uniform. He had the weary resignation about him that bespoke a former soldier. Eogan would have to be watchful of him.

Barton was the first to speak. "Why did they want you dead?"

"I could ask you the same thing." Eogan tightened his fingers on his gun. "If what you say is true, then you were also set up in that ambush."

Barton nodded. "They must have found out I was working against them. I'd joined H.R.F. several months ago. Most of my team were members."

"What is the H.R.F.?" Eogan asked. He had already knew, but he wanted Barton's explanation.

"It stands for the Human Resistance Force." Barton lifted his chin. "Our goal is to protect the human race from extraterrestrials."

"So they knew you were a traitor." Eogan nodded. "They suspected that I would also betray them."

"How?" Barton frowned. "They spoke as if they had you under control, almost as if you were a weapon."

"Do you know who I am?"

Barton shook his head. "They wouldn't say. My orders were to keep you in sight and not give you a gun."

"I do not need a firearm to kill." Eogan's voice was matter of fact. "I am a Hunter. We are bred and trained from birth to be the best warriors in the universe."

The older man's eyes widened. "I thought Hunters were a myth."

"I am real." Eogan glanced at Barton. "They captured me when I was fifteen and inserted implants to control me. They have used me to do their bidding for the last thirty years, but no more."

"Why the change?" The older man's voice was suspicious.

"I discovered I had been lied to. I thought I was the only Hunter on Earth and with the controls they had in place, I was forced to comply. I was bred to obey and even without the implants, following orders is what a Hunter does."

"You could have escaped," Barton said.

"Why?" Eogan knew these men wouldn't understand the need to follow commands. It was what he'd been genetically modified and trained to do. He had always observed the Sacred Code and fought with honor. "One master is the same as another. Besides, I am not from this planet."

"You're an alien?" The younger man's voice held disbelief. "You look human."

"And my genes say I am human." Eogan looked back at Barton. "Six months ago I found out that there was a unit of Hunters stranded on Earth. That is when I made my plans to leave."

"What made them suspect you?"

"They had captured another Hunter and his mate. I helped them escape." Eogan shrugged. "They couldn't prove it, but they had their suspicions."

Captain Barton nodded. "So they thought they would test you."

"The mission was an ambush. They hoped that I would die trying to defeat the enemy."

"Or you would run." Barton finished in a dry voice.

The older man frowned and pointed at Hester. "What about her?"

"She is my pair bond."

Eogan didn't hesitate to admit what Hester was to him. He had no doubts. He had bonded to her and the link would be there for the rest of his life. They might never be mates, but the connection between them would always exist.

Captain Barton rose an eyebrow. "I don't understand."

Hester cleared her throat. "He rescued me from some men who had shot three of my companions and were about to rape me."

"I killed them." Eogan spoke without emotion. "They had broken the Sacred Code, and the punishment is death."

"That doesn't explain why you were in Incirlik." Barton asked. "Was it because you murdered those people and they captured you?"

"It's my fault." Hester shook her bag. "They had planted a transmitter on me and used it to follow me. They only took Eogan because he insisted on coming with me."

"You volunteered?" The older man's voice rose.

"It is my duty to protect Hester." Eogan didn't understand why the man should be surprised. "I knew she would need my help to escape."

"Why did they want you?" Barton turned his gaze to Hester.

"They thought I was part of your H.R.F. organization." She shrugged. "One minute I'm talking to someone I met on the internet about Gobekli Tepe, and the next they're shooting at me."

"So that brings us back to our original question. How did you escape?" Barton crossed his arms. "That's a protected base. No one leaves it. We've been trying for months to figure a way in."

"Getting in is easy." Eogan's voice was matter of fact. "Get yourself captured."

The older man snorted. "You sound like you have a death wish."

"I do not fear it. A Hunter is bred to fight. Death is the inevitable result of battle."

"We're not going on a suicide mission." The younger man's voice was filled with exasperation. "I don't want to die."

"No one does." Captain Barton's tone was soothing. "We are fighting so that others can live."

"What are you battling exactly?" Hester's voice held confusion.

"We are determined to defeat the aliens who have taken over our planet."

"The Albireons." Eogan nodded. "They are the scourge of the universe. It was foolish of your leaders to let them stay."

"Who are you to judge?" The older man glared at him. "You have been working with them for over thirty years."

"Human handlers gave me my orders and controlled me against my will." Eogan's voice was a low threat. "No Hunter would willingly stand beside an Albireon. We have fought many wars on other planets to defeat them."

The younger man took a step forward and shook his clenched fist at Eogan. "How dare you suggest that we want them here?"

Eogan readied his weapon. "It was not a suggestion, but a fact. Your leaders let them set up laboratories and do experiments on this planet in exchange for technological knowledge. The Albireons have had seventy years to consolidate their position on Earth, and soon they will destroy it."

"Do you know this for certain?" Captain Barton spoke in a reasonable tone as he pushed the younger man back.

"It is what they do," Eogan said. "The other Hunters on Earth have fought them more than once. They know that they have financial, communication, and technological control of this planet. It is only a matter of time before they show their real motive."

"What is their purpose?" The older man's eyes narrowed.

"They will decimate the human race and all living organisms on this planet."

There was silence for a few seconds after Eogan's declaration. He could tell by the look on the men's faces they didn't trust what he'd told them. They might have suspected the Albireons had an ulterior motive for being on Earth, but nothing this devastating.

"We knew they were experimenting on humans and kidnapping them, but our surveillance hasn't led us to believe they want to destroy us." Captain Barton was the first to speak.

"It is what they have done on other planets. They harvest genes and then annihilate the populace so that they have a monopoly on the genome. They sell and trade in genetics."

"That's horrible." The young man's voice was a high squeak. "What kind of monsters are they?"

Eogan debated whether to tell them what he had recently learned and then decided that they had the right to know. He'd overheard snippets of conversation about the experiments taking place in the lower levels of Pine Gap over the years. Usually it was about the people unaccounted for and missing. In recent months, it had been about the number of bodies preserved in suspended animation.

The soldiers who frequented the Albireon areas were appalled at the sight of tubes running in and out of these humans. Eogan had suspected that the Albireons were producing a chemical from the bodies. He'd overheard a discussion between General Carter and another officer that had confirmed his suspicions. The Albireons were in the testing stages of a drug that had the potential to make them rich. Little did his handlers realize that the Albireons would never let a single human live when they were finished with their experiments.

"It is far more devastating. They have discovered that some of your hormonal secretions can be modified into a designer drug that other species will pay a fortune for. The human genome is priceless to them. They can't risk letting anyone else in the universe discover or own it."

"They'll use us for synthesizing drugs?" Hester shivered. "That's horrible."

"They will utilize the genes they have gathered to recombine into humans that produce vast amounts of the hormones they need for their drug. What is left of your race will be nothing more than a manufacturing machine."

"How can any species do that to another?"

Eogan sensed Hester's revulsion. He wanted to protect her from the horror of the Albireons, but she needed to know the truth. It was the only way to save humanity from the fate that the Albireons had planned.

"The Albireons are a race that cares about control and status. Money gives them both. If they can produce a drug that other races become addicted to, then they will have power over all planets and species."

"It makes sense, in a sick way." Barton's voice was filled with disgust. "That means it's even more important that the H.R.F. carry out its agenda."

"What are your plans?" Eogan asked.

"We are determined to destroy the Albireons and Albirsion Corporation." Barton lifted his chin. "You are a warrior and have knowledge of them. Will you help us?"

"I cannot speak for all Hunters only myself."

"What is your decision?"

Eogan looked at Hester. She was biting her lower lip, and he sensed her indecision. The Albireons meant all humans harm, and it was his duty to protect her. It didn't matter whether the battle was an honorable one or if it was inevitable. All that concerned him was what was best for Hester.

She glanced up at him and for a brief second he saw the outrage and anger in her eyes. There was no fear about the outcome. Infuriation that the Albireons had been allowed to live on earth without being stopped, raced through her. He understood her fury.

The Albireons were a parasite upon the planet and the universe.

He made his decision.

"I will help you with your fight."

Chapter 18

Eogan surveyed the farm on the outskirts of Adana that they had been transported to. It was quaint, with a few outbuildings and a house. There were no animals outside, and the garden was overgrown with weeds. A perfect place to hide. No one would think it was inhabited, especially not by a group of resistance fighters.

He sensed Hester's uncertainty about trusting these men.

Eogan reached for her hand and squeezed it. He sent her comfort and reassurance. She was finding it strange that he was able to know what she was thinking and feeling. He could only hope that in time, she would accept it. Right now, she was afraid. She didn't show it on the outside, but inside, she was scared. After a few seconds, he sensed her relax.

They had escaped from one of the most secure bases in the world. He would not fail her now.

He sent out a mind connect to Ardal. *"We are arriving at the Human Resistance Force's headquarters. It is an abandoned farm outside of Adana, and undetectable from the air."*

"Let us know the exact location so we can prepare to help if necessary."

Ardal's voice was firm. When Eogan had communicated with him after agreeing to assist the H.R.F., Ardal had been in agreement. The Albireons must be defeated. It was their duty as Hunters to rid Earth of this scourge. They would proceed with caution though.

"I will give them the information they want about the Albireons' defenses at the base, and then make my decision about how far to continue with them."

"I trust your judgement. You have more experience dealing with security issues on this planet. Do not endanger your life. Wait for us, and we will finish the operation without the H.R.F. if necessary."

Eogan had his instructions.

If these humans were trustworthy, then the full force of the Hunters on Earth would support them in their cause. Otherwise, Ardal and his unit of warriors, would battle the Albireons on their own, as previously planned.

He had to decide if the H.R.F. would be a worthy ally or a

hindrance in the fight against the Albireons. The H.R.F. wanted to know details about the inside of the base and how they could launch a strike at it. It had seemed a simple enough idea to help them. It would be a disaster to proceed with an attack if they were not prepared.

The covered van they were riding in drove into a stone outbuilding and stopped. Hester frowned and looked at him. A shiver went through her. Her fear became his as it coursed through him. She wasn't comfortable with this arrangement. He sent her reassurance. The H.R.F. were taking the necessary precautions against an enemy that was better equipped and unrelenting in their pursuit.

"The building protects us from detection and airborne surveillance." He leaned close so that only Hester could hear his words.

She straightened her shoulders and stepped out of the vehicle.

"We'll take the tunnels now." Barton's voice was low. "That's the only way to join the rest of the group."

Captain Barton motioned them to follow the older associate, who they now knew was called Simon. The younger man, Robert, reversed the van and drove away. Eogan watched him as he turned onto the road and headed in the direction of the city. If there was a tracking device on the vehicle, they would monitor him. He reached for Hester's hand and brought her close. Everything about this place spoke subterfuge and secrecy.

"Are you certain you want to do this?" Eogan asked.

"What choice do we have?" She looked up at him. "This is our only option if the human race is going to be destroyed."

"You don't have to go with me." Eogan couldn't bear the thought of something happening to Hester. "I will take you to the other Hunters and come back and help with the battle."

Hester shook her head. "I'm continuing with you."

"Once we meet with these people, you will be labeled a rebel." Eogan's tone was serious. He had to impress upon her the consequences of her staying.

"The Albireons have bugged my backpack, held me captive, and threatened me with torture. I think they already consider me a dissident. At least now I'll have earned the title." Hester's voice was dry.

"You'll be a fugitive forever."

"Isn't that what you are?" Hester glanced up at him. "If we're bonded, then whatever happens to you, affects me."

Eogan clenched his jaw and nodded.

She turned away and followed Simon.

Eogan couldn't fault her reasoning. He was already a fugitive, and was being hunted by the Albireons and the humans who worked for them. The only thing that could change the reality of his future was to defeat the Albireons. For Hester's sake, he would succeed.

He joined her at the entrance to the tunnel and gave her hand a reassuring squeeze.

There was a long wooden ladder that had been lowered into a round cement tube that led underground. No bottom was visible. Eogan went first so that he could guide Hester's feet on the rungs. When they reached the end of the ladder, battery powered lights flickered a stream of illumination on the area. The lights were placed at intervals throughout a narrow, winding tunnel. He could make out the stone walls and dirt floor that they were traveling over. The ground slanted downward, sending them even deeper underground.

"*I will be with you always*," Eogan whispered into Hester's mind. She looked up at him and smiled. Their bond was strengthening.

After ten minutes, the tunnel opened up into a wide space. From this central area other tunnels branched out in five different directions. It was an underground labyrinth. Eogan glanced over his shoulder. Behind him the tunnel they had come through was now dark. His eyesight was improved on Earth and he could make out the faint shadows of people standing just beyond the other tunnel entrances. His guess was that they were armed and waiting for them to make a false move.

"Welcome." A vibrant male's voice greeted them from the darkness. "I'm glad that Barton was able to persuade you to visit."

Eogan crossed his arms. "You have need of our help."

"It would be appreciated." A man who was about forty years old came into the light. He was tall with graying black hair, and a long scar down the right side of his cheek. "I am Hank Davis."

Hank held his hand out to him. He took it after a few seconds. "I am Eogan."

"I've heard of you." Hank's eyes narrowed. "There were reports that the Security Division had a specialized killer."

"I was bred and trained to be a warrior."

"There were also rumors that you were not from Earth." Hank's voice became harsh. "If that is the case, why should we trust you?"

"I think it's more a question of me trusting you." Eogan lifted an eyebrow. "Your men approached us and asked for help."

Hank nodded. "You're right. Could you at least tell me why you'd be willing to aid us?"

"I crash landed here when I was fifteen and was captured by the Albireon allies. They have held me in captivity since then. I have no love for them."

Hank considered this for a few seconds and then turned to Hester. "And you must be Dr. Adams. Steve Jackson mentioned that you had been in communication with him. I hope you found everything you were searching for."

"It's been an enlightening experience." Hester didn't bother to hide her sarcasm. "Steve didn't tell me that he was connected with the H.R.F. I take it you are in charge?"

"I started the Human Resistance Force and lead it. Steve contacted us via the internet. He'd found evidence of aliens on the planet and was meeting with you to discuss this further."

"Your communications are being monitored," Eogan said. "There was an ambush set up for Hester and her companions. Steve and Franklin are in Incirlik still. They abandoned her to their attackers."

Hank sighed. "Franklin is one of our newer recruits. I'm afraid he isn't well trained."

"He has no honor."

Hank gave a crooked smile. "That's a term I haven't heard in many years. Unfortunately, we have to accept everyone who comes to us. There is a great need for people who believe us and are willing to fight the Albireon threat."

"How do you know about the Albireons?" Eogan's eyes narrowed. "Few people alive have seen them."

"Yet here we both are." Hank sighed. "I used to work for Albirsion Corporation. I was a Major in the US Marines and when I retired, I accepted a job with what I thought was a private security group. Little did I realize I was working for aliens."

"You killed for them." Eogan's words were a statement.

"As did you."

"I had implants and tracking devices."

"And I thought that I was helping my country. When I realized what was happening, I escaped. I've been on the run ever since."

"So we are both men of honor who were deceived."

Hank tilted his head. "The question is, are you willing to help us defeat them?"

Eogan glanced around at the other people who had gathered. There were about fifty, men and women, most of them carrying weapons. He hoped more were waiting in the tunnels than he could see, because they would need more soldiers to overtake a military base.

"I am a Hunter, an elite warrior, sworn to uphold the Sacred Code. The Albireons have broken this code, and the penalty is death. I and my fellow Hunters will fight to defeat them and rid this planet of their presence."

There was silence after Eogan's statement.

Hank Davis was the first to recover. "There are more of you on Earth?"

Eogan nodded. "Others have crashed here and have been working to bring justice to those who ask for it. They are aware of the Albireon threat and have taken measures to sabotage their operations."

"What actions?" Hank's voice sounded dazed.

"They have infiltrated their financial stranglehold on this planet's banks. From there they will be able to penetrate their communications and computer networks."

"What else have they planned?"

"Once I join with them, we will start to destroy their hiding places." Eogan shrugged. "Albireons have to be hunted and exterminated."

"Will they work with us?" Hank motioned to the people surrounding him. "Or do we run two separate campaigns against them?"

"It is good that humans are prepared to fight."

"So we should set up a coordinated effort."

"That is the usual approach." Eogan crossed his arm. "I have informed Ardal, the leader of the Hunters, of your existence."

"How many Hunters can we count on?"

"Enough to do the job," Eogan said. "We are in hiding from the Albireons and other human agencies. It would be foolish of me to give these details to people I have just met."

Hank hesitated then nodded. "You're right. On the same note, I am unprepared to give the details of our network."

"Understood." Eogan glanced behind his shoulder. "You can tell the people you have hiding that it is unnecessary to hold their weapons on us."

Hank inhaled a sharp breath. "You can see them?"

"I can also sense their presence. It is a logical strategy to ensure that we were not going to attack, but it is distressing my pair bond and I cannot allow that."

Hester took a step closer to him.

Hank glanced over at her. "We're all uncomfortable. Don't tell me you're going to attack us just because Dr. Adams is anxious."

"I have sworn with the sacred oath of a Hunter that I will protect her. Have them stand down."

Hank shrugged. "Get used to it."

Eogan's eyes narrowed. This human did not understand the full significance of the pair bond, and there was no point wasting time explaining. He pushed Hester behind him and grabbed the man on his right. He disarmed him and then used his captive as a shield as he moved back against a wall and swung the assault rifle in an arc. If he'd been firing, everyone in the hall would have been dead.

His movement was so quick that none of them had time to react.

"I could have killed all of you. Instead, I've shown you the worth of my vow."

Hank's reach for his firearm was stopped midair.

A muscle twitched in his jaw.

"I have no reason to trust you." Eogan trained the gun on Hank. "I've been imprisoned and controlled by humans just like you, except they're still working with the Albireons. I will not hesitate to kill in order to protect Hester."

Eogan watched as Hank struggled with the decision of whether to trust him. He couldn't blame the man for being cautious. He didn't fully trust H.R.F. either. Albireons had altered his implants and held him prisoner, but humans had been responsible for the killing missions that he'd been forced to do. It had also been humans that had captured him when he was fifteen.

After a few seconds, Hank nodded. "Lower your weapons and come out."

Ten men, all armed with machine guns, exited the tunnels surrounding them.

"I won't be treated like a prisoner if we are to work together." Eogan's voice was harsh. "Remember, you came to me for help."

Hank held up his hands in a conciliatory gesture. "Calm down.

Our weapons are away. There is no need to be suspicious."

Eogan released the man he was holding and lowered the weapon.

He took a step away from the wall and Hester walked out from behind him. She straightened her jacket and put the strap of her pack over one of her shoulders before grinning up at him. His heart eased. She hadn't been upset by his actions. Instead, they had seemed to reassure her that he was in control of this situation and no harm would come to her.

"We talk as equals, or this discussion is over." This was the only way that Ardal and the other Hunters would consider allying themselves with these people.

"As you wish." Hank gave him a lopsided grin. "The rumors about your abilities weren't even close to the truth."

"We are the best warriors in the universe. We are brothers and to make an enemy of one of us is a mistake."

"I can see that." Hank looked at Hester. "I meant no disrespect by my comments."

"Eogan takes his protection very seriously." Hester said. "He saved my life when Steve and Franklin ran. I didn't ask to be involved in this. I wanted to explore Gobekli Tepe and maybe have a few crazy discussions about its possible link to aliens. I didn't plan to be taking part in a battle against an alien race."

"None of us planned it." Hank motioned for the lights in the tunnels to be turned on. "This is a war that has been thrust upon us."

"Just as long as you remember that Eogan is not the enemy. Neither of us needs to be here."

A jolt of surprise shot through Eogan.

Hester was shielding him.

Never in forty-five years, had anyone protected him. It was a new and exhilarating experience. A Hunter didn't need or expect praise when they did their duty. Hester's approval and defense of him sent a thrill of satisfaction throughout him. It energized him. For the first time, he was eager to do battle. The sooner he defeated the Albireons, the quicker he could get Hester to safety.

"The easiest way to get onto the base is to be captured." Eogan handed Hank the gun he had confiscated. "My suggestion is that you turn me in."

Chapter 19

Hester's breath caught in her throat.

She couldn't lose Eogan. She'd only just found him.

"That's too dangerous." She grabbed his arm. "They'll kill you."

"They can try." Eogan lowered his voice. "I will be prepared."

"You two might want to discuss this first." Hank's voice was dry.

"There is no need. I will be the entry onto the base." Eogan motioned to the others. "After that, you would have to open the gates for your fellow H.R.F. members. Together, we will destroy the Albireons."

Eogan's words were cutting a hole in her heart. He was deliberately putting himself in danger and relying on the H.R.F. to free him. She started to shake at the thought of losing Eogan. He was trained to put his life on the line, but she couldn't let him go. What if he didn't return? She couldn't tolerate even the thought of never seeing him again.

"*I will be with you always, even in death.*" The words were a soft whisper inside her mind. "*There is no need to fear. Trust me.*"

Hester took a deep breath and released her anxiety. She had to believe Eogan knew what he was doing. He had saved her from the impossible already. He would be able to defeat the Albireons.

Hank nodded. "I like the idea. We have to work out the details."

"A night attack would be best."

Hank looked down at the watch on his wrist. "That gives us another twelve hours to prepare. It will be difficult to coordinate everything in that time."

"Eogan needs rest." Hester spoke in a fierce voice. Eogan looked at her with surprise, but she didn't care. "You were up all night standing guard. To be in top form, you need sleep."

She lifted her chin and stared back at him.

A second later he nodded. "I will rest and then we'll discuss the plans your team has put in place."

"Agreed."

"First I must give these to Captain Barton." Eogan reached into the top pocket of his jacket and pulled out a stack of patches. "These are the name tags of the fallen soldiers from the Akcakale raid."

Barton took them from Eogan. "Thank you. I will inform their families."

Eogan turned to Hank. "We are ready."

Hank motioned to one of the women beside him. "Lena will show you to a room where you can sleep. We'll talk later."

Lena looked to be in her late thirties, with long, brown hair pulled back into a ponytail. She wore green, military fatigues, a tan t-shirt, and a camouflage vest. Her hazel eyes were alert and wary as she holstered her pistol. She took them down one of the side tunnels which opened up every twenty feet to smaller rooms. She stopped after about five minutes and ushered them into a cave-like enclosure. It had several large cushions on the ground and a couple of folded, gray blankets on top of them.

"I'll be back with some food and water." She pulled a curtain across the entrance giving them the illusion of privacy.

Hester was about to speak when Eogan put a finger to his lips. He reached a hand up and started to feel along the walls of the oval room. He patted down the hardened, earth walls until he had covered every inch of the room. He did the same to the floor before he shook out the cushions. When he was satisfied that they weren't being bugged, he held his arms open to her.

She sank into his embrace and let his nearness ease her. Serenity replaced tension. So much had happened since yesterday that it seemed more like a dream than reality. Eogan was the only thing that grounded her. She luxuriated in the calm and comfort his presence gave her.

Lena came back a few minutes later with some water, bread, and hard cheese. It was simple and delicious. She and Eogan sat on the ground and ate in silence. Too much had happened between them for mundane chit-chat. Hester just wanted to enjoy her first meal with Eogan in peace. There would be time to talk afterwards.

When they were finished, she gathered the plates together and placed them outside the entrance. She turned back to Eogan, who had arranged the cushions into a bed. He patted one and motioned to her.

"You need sleep."

"Look who's talking? You haven't slept in days."

"I will relax when I know you are safe."

Hester knelt beside him. "I don't want you injured."

Her voice shook and tears pricked at her eyes. They had gone from one danger to another, and this proposal of using himself as bait, was by far the worse threat to his life. No one was tracking them now. There was nothing to prevent them from leaving and starting fresh somewhere else.

"We would never be free." Eogan had read her thoughts once again. "I am a warrior. I must do what is right."

Hester swallowed back her tears. "I've been alone my whole life, and I'd grown used to it. I never expected to find someone. All that changed with you."

"It has been the same for me." Eogan kept his voice low. "Hunters were forbidden to mate and our implants made certain that we never did. I never imagined I would know the joy of bonding with another."

"So we're the same." Hester leaned her head on his chest. "I don't want to lose that."

"If I don't stop the Albireons now, we'll never live in peace." Eogan's voice was gruff. "We might blend in on this planet, but the Albireons will make certain that you are never able to see your parents or return to your job at the university."

"My life would be pointless without you." Hester's voice was a whisper. "You are my other half. I never thought anything as intense as bonding was possible. I want to spend the rest of my life with you."

Eogan's eyes widened. "Are you telling me you will be my mate?"

Hester nodded.

"I dared not hope that you would desire me for a mate. We are bonded, but you have the right to choose another." Eogan's voice was hoarse. "It is an honor that you wish to be mated with me."

She smiled. "I think you're pretty terrific too. That's why I don't want you getting killed in this raid."

"It is hard to kill a Hunter."

"Promise?"

Eogan nodded and pulled her close. She could feel his breath on her cheek and her heart started to beat at a frantic pace. She sensed that he was going to kiss her, and she licked her dry lips. His eyes widened and then his head lowered to hers.

It was a soft, tentative brush of lips.

Heat rushed through her.

She leaned closer, straining every muscle in her body to be nearer to him. He wrapped his arms around her back and supported her as he deepened the kiss. Sparks of fire tingled everywhere. Eogan's tongue slid against hers, gliding and tasting, as they lost themselves in each other.

Time ceased to matter and the world spun away. Her essence touched his as they sealed their bond. The rattle of their dishes being picked up outside, broke the spell. They parted. Hester opened her eyes to find Eogan staring down at her with a blazing intensity.

"That was my first kiss." She inhaled a sharp breath. "I never knew it could be so beautiful."

"You gave me a glimpse of paradise." Eogan brushed her hair from her face. "Why has no man kissed you before?"

"Nobody ever wanted me." Hester's voice was matter of fact. Her memories of rejection and loneliness had disappeared with Eogan's kiss. "I'm glad I waited. Anything else would have been a disappointment."

"We are bonded physically, mentally, and spiritually. It is a connection that nothing can sever. I will always feel and hear you, no matter where you are."

"That's comforting. Will I be able to do the same?"

"In time." Eogan sighed. "Understand, I am willing to fight because that is the only way you and I will be together."

Hester nodded. "I trust you to stay safe."

He stretched out on the makeshift bed and patted the cushion. "Let me hold you in sleep."

She reached for the blanket and spread it out before she lay beside Eogan. He pulled her close and rested her head on his shoulder. Contentment and joy filled her. This was where she always wanted to be. Held in Eogan's arms. Now they were to be mated and no one could ever separate them again. The thought of it added to her happiness.

"If we're going to be mates does that mean we're now engaged?"

"It means whatever you wish." Eogan kissed the top of her head. "What is engaged?"

"When two people promise to marry and spend the rest of their lives together, they are engaged."

"Then we are engaged."

"I can't believe it." Hester yawned. "You do want to marry me?"

"Yes."

She snuggled closer. Her eyes closed as Eogan's arms tightened around her. He was right. She was exhausted. He knew so much more about her than she realized. With startling clarity, she recognized that she could sense just as much about Eogan. He was weary, yet he wouldn't rest until he'd freed the planet from the Albireons' clutches.

He'd spent too many years a prisoner and puppet for them. To stop them from destroying Earth was necessary for him. It was the only way he would heal from the mental scars their imprisonment had left on him. Her last thought before she drifted off to sleep was that in order for Eogan to be whole, she needed to let him help the H.R.F. That was the only way he would have peace.

She was alone when she woke.

Confusion filled her as she looked around the darkened cave-like room. The pillows beneath her were rumpled, and when she put her hand on the cushion beside her, it was cold. That meant Eogan had left some time ago. At least he'd gotten some rest.

She sat and stretched her arms in the air. She picked up her bag and stood. What if Eogan had gone on the mission without telling her? A flicker of fear and a sense of abandonment surged through her. Surely he wouldn't have done that. Not after their discussion before she'd fallen asleep in his embrace.

She reached out to him with her mind. *"Where are you?"*

No answer came back.

Panic filled her.

At that moment, she heard footsteps rushing down the tunnel. They stopped outside of the curtain that was pulled over the door to their room. Someone cleared their throat and Hester opened the drape. Lena stood waiting. Hester eased the tension in her shoulders.

"Eogan requested that I bring you to him."

She nodded and followed the woman back to the central area where they had first met Hank Davis. A large group of people were gathered around a map that was pinned up on one of the walls. When she entered, Eogan turned and smiled. He held his hand out to her, and she grabbed it.

Peace.

Contentment.

The world righted itself, and all it took was standing beside Eogan.

He hadn't forgotten her. When she'd reached out to him with her mind, he'd heard and made certain she was taken care of. It was a novel experience to have someone concerned about her welfare. It was one she never thought she would have, and that made it all the more precious. She hugged her happiness close as she turned to the map on the wall.

It was Incirlik base.

Hank Davis was pointing to the first checkpoint. "This is where we'll make our demands to see the person in charge."

"We can't guarantee they'll let us in," Simon said.

"Tell them you've captured me. That will get their attention." Eogan's voice was matter of fact. "We should all be arrested then."

"What's the plan if they only take you?" Hank asked.

Eogan shrugged. "Then I will defeat them on my own."

"That's crazy." Hank punched a finger on the map. "We will force them to take all of us. It's too much to ask one man to fight a whole military base."

"Tell them you're going to go public about the Albireons. They'll have no choice but to arrest all of you," Hester said.

"She's right," Eogan agreed. "Once you threaten them, you are a risk."

Eogan's approval wrapped around her like a hug.

"Then we'll do it." Hank's voice was decisive. "They can't expect to control all of us."

"If you show up at the gate with twenty people, they won't let you in." Captain Barton had been standing at the edge of the crowd. He walked up to the map. "It would be best if we could have one person go in, and then somehow free themselves so that they could let the rest of us into the base."

Barton's plan had merit.

"Maybe you should take it a step further. If you overtake the people at the guardhouse when you first arrive, then none of you will be held captive," Hester suggested.

"We'll storm the gate and continue to move through the base until we've taken the area where the subterranean levels are located." Hank pursed his lips as he considered the strategy.

"Too risky." Eogan frowned. "It would be better if you let them take me alone if necessary. When I reach the second gatehouse, I will break free. Have your people waiting near that location. I'll destroy the fence so they can enter."

"It's messy," Barton objected. "I say we do this at night. The darkness will help us. Two people should take Eogan into the Incirlik. I am the logical person. As far as they know I survived the ambush on the border and am just returning from my mission with a prisoner."

"I need to be there." Hank's voice was decisive. "Once we are inside, the others should be able to cut the wire and enter the base."

"It is not wise for you to go with me." Eogan shook his head. "You are the commander and should be with the rest of your men to lead them in the assault. We will meet up with you at the hangar that hides the underground structure."

"This is my group. I say what happens."

Simon stepped forward. "We shouldn't have our leadership all in one place. If something goes wrong, we need to know that the H.R.F. will survive. I will go with them."

Hank took a few seconds to consider Simon's option and then nodded. "Okay."

"You'll be there for the fighting," Eogan assured. "Now, we need to plan the logistics of the attack. Barton, Simon, and I will go in when it's dark. If they refuse to let anyone accompany me onto the base, then Simon and Barton will join the others."

"What will you do if you're alone?" Hank crossed his arms and frowned. "You can't possibly overtake all those men."

"I'll attack once I'm in the hangar. I will not kill them because I may need information." Eogan's voice was unemotional. "We need to gain access to the secret weapons that are hidden on the base. This base is similar to Pine Gap, but the weapons may be in another location. I will need one of the soldiers to tell me the location."

"This is the first time we're hearing about needing special armaments." Simon sounded wary. "Surely we have enough to attack?"

"The Albireons have regenerative abilities. They may survive a bullet. This is not a normal firearm, but a direct energy weapon."

A shiver went through Hester at the cold determination she heard in Eogan's voice.

"We need it to eradicate the Albireons."

Simon's eyes narrowed. "I've never heard of it."

"It's a laser-induced plasma stream." Eogan's tone was matter of fact. "It will produce a high heat that will ensure that no Albireon is left alive."

"Like an electro-laser?" Simon took a step back. "I thought those were still in the experimental stages."

"There were rumors about specialized ordnances. Are you positive it exists?" Hank asked.

Eogan nodded. "Explosives would be better, but there is no time. We have to ensure there are no Albireons left alive at Incirlik."

"Once you get the weapon, then what?" Hank had turned back to the map. "We'll be coming in from the western side and can meet you in the hangar."

"The area has to be secured without a battle." Eogan pointed to the map. "This is restricted from the rest of the base. The regular personnel probably don't know what happens here."

"We're in and out with as little disruption as possible." Hank nodded. "Is it wise to leave witnesses?"

"We only want to kill the Albireons." Eogan's voice was stern. "We must minimize the number of humans killed."

"So, this is a covert operation to engage the Albireons only." Hank crossed his arms over his chest.

"No warnings must leave the area. We can't risk fighting the men and weapons available to the whole base," Captain Barton added. "When we have the guards under control, Simon you'll be responsible for keeping the prisoners contained and silent."

"Done." Simon's voice was firm.

"That will leave Barton and Eogan to overtake the rest," Hank said.

"We'll use the element of surprise." Eogan turned away from the map. "We should be ready to go in an hour."

The rest of the people scattered, leaving Hester alone with Eogan.

His face was set in stern lines and she sensed that he was preparing himself for the mission ahead. It wouldn't be easy, but if anyone could do it, Eogan could.

"Will I be with you, or with the others waiting at the fence?" Hester was getting anxious about the coming battle. There was no way she was going to let Eogan go in there without her.

Eogan shook his head. "You are staying here with some of the women and younger recruits."

"No." She jutted out her chin. "Where you go, I go."

"Not this time." A muscle twitched in Eogan's jaw. "I need to know that you are safe. The only way I can be certain, is for you to stay here."

"You would never stay away if I were in danger."

"True, but I am a warrior. I have been trained for this since birth." Eogan's voice softened. "You are my mate and there is nothing in the world I wouldn't do to protect you, including die. If I know you are safe, then I can focus on the upcoming battle."

"I want to be with you." Hester wasn't giving up this argument.

Eogan gathered her close. "If you insist, then I will honor your wishes because that is what I am trained to do. I desire that you stay here. Otherwise, I won't be able to do my job."

She hesitated. Eogan needed to concentrate on the battle ahead. If he found her presence a distraction, then that might make it more difficult for him to fight. She would never forgive herself if she were responsible for him being injured, or worse, killed. She knew nothing about weapons or fighting. The sensible thing was for her to remain here.

As much as it pained her to think of him facing so many enemies alone, she had to do what he asked.

She looked up at him. "I will stay."

Chapter 20

Night had fallen and the rest of the team was in place.

Eogan took a deep breath and eased the tension from his neck. Battle was upon them. Hester was safe so he could focus on the task ahead. The base was well protected and yet he knew there were weaknesses in its security. Nothing was impenetrable. He would find the surveillance flaws as he moved through the battle. It was what a Hunter did best, strategize on the go.

Ardal's men had not arrived.

He could wait no longer.

"*We are going in.*" He sent the mind connection to Ardal. "*If your men arrive in time, they will find us at the northwest hangar.*"

"*Understood.*"

Eogan broke the connection. He was capable of handling this battle on his own. Help from the other Hunters would be appreciated, but it wasn't necessary to destroy the Albireons. The underground area was similar to Pine Gap and he was very familiar with it. Finding the enemy wouldn't be a problem.

Barton was driving the truck they were traveling in. He still wore the uniform he'd been in when Eogan had first met him two nights ago. He looked as if he'd survived a battle, which was part of the plan.

He glanced over at Eogan. "Ready?"

Eogan nodded. "It is time. The others should be in place."

"Let's do this." Simon's voice sounded determined.

Tonight was the beginning of the battle for Earth.

This was the first nest of Albireons to be hit, and Eogan was determined to rid this base of the extraterrestrials. Humans deserved the right to live without the threat of genetic harvesting and genocide. Barton shifted the truck into gear and headed for the first guardhouse.

There were two men in uniform waiting as they pulled up.

Barton handed over his credentials. "I have two prisoners."

The guard looked at the papers and then up at Barton. "This says you have special clearance. Where are you going?"

"I report to General Carter."

The guard's eyebrows rose. "That's a restricted zone." He pointed to the area. "You will have to go through the second clearance gate to reach it."

"Understood." Barton took back his papers and waited for the gate to be lifted before driving through.

He exhaled a loud breath when they had driven beyond the gate. "Maybe we won't have to overpower the second set of guards."

"We need to ensure that no alarms are activated." Eogan's eyes narrowed. "I am surprised that they let you go through so easily."

"General Carter was the only one who knew about the mission we were sent on." Barton slowed as they reached the second gate. "I doubt anyone here would be aware that it was a deliberate ambush designed to kill all of us."

"He thought that was easier than announcing you were a traitor?" Simon's voice held doubt.

"You do not know Carter." Eogan's voice was dry. "The man is sadistic. Whatever causes the most pain, and the least paperwork, would be his preferred method."

Barton snorted. "You must have worked with him for many years."

"Ten." Eogan forced back his revulsion. "The man has no honor."

"Then it is past time that we paid him back with some of his own medicine." Barton grinned. "Ready boys?"

They stopped at the gate.

Another two guards came out to meet them. One circled the truck and looked into the passenger's window. His nametag identified him as Foster. His eyes narrowed as he scanned the truck's interior. Eogan took a deep breath and prepared for battle.

His partner reached for Barton's papers.

"I'll have to call for clearance." The second guard took the paperwork and went back into the guardhouse.

Barton looked at Eogan.

Eogan nodded and leaned out his window and grabbed Foster's weapon. At the same time, he pulled him close and slammed his head into the truck frame. The man went limp.

Barton opened his door. The other guard stepped out of the small guard building to stop him, but Barton was quicker. He hit him over the head with the butt of his pistol. The guard fell backwards into the guardhouse. Simon followed Barton out of the truck, and Eogan opened his door, grabbing Foster and dragging him into the guard house.

Simon was punching code into the computer and unbuttoning his shirt. Barton stripped Foster and handed Simon the uniform. Several seconds later, Simon was dressed as a guard and in control of the computers. The two unconscious guards were gagged and handcuffed to a metal strut in the building.

"In case they wake before we're done."

Simon picked up a weapon. "The cameras overlooking the hangar and the fence are on a loop."

"That should give us enough time before an alarm is raised."

"I'll stay here until Hank and his reinforcements arrive. Then I'll join you."

Barton gripped Simon's shoulder. "Good luck."

Simon nodded and turned back to the computers. Barton and Eogan left the guard post and climbed back into the truck. It had taken only a few minutes for them to overcome the guards and take over. Luckily no one had approached them. Now they had to complete the mission.

Barton started the truck and drove to the hangar. "We should have enough time before an alarm is raised."

"We need to secure the hangar before the others arrive." Eogan pulled a pistol out from under the seat and checked the magazine. "There will be at least two security officers guarding the entrance and then possibly more at the elevators to the underground area."

"What's the plan?" Barton's hands tightened on the steering wheel.

Eogan wanted to minimize human deaths as much as possible. It was unrealistic to expect no casualties, though. If they met with resistance, then they would have to use whatever force was necessary. They had to meet their objective.

"Once inside the hangar, keep driving until you can't go any further." Eogan grabbed the door handle. "You should be able to draw some of the guards your way."

"What about you?"

"I'll jump to safety and then take out the men that are a problem."

Barton gave him a long look before nodding. "We'll meet at the elevators."

"Agreed."

Eogan waited until they had reached the large sliding doors at the entrance to the hangar. Just as a guard came out to stop them, he opened the truck door and jumped out. That was Barton's signal to gun the vehicle.

Barton sped through the open hangar doors before anyone could stop him.

Eogan hit the pavement on his side and rolled to a stop in front of the first guard. He kicked him in the leg. There was the unmistakable sound of a bone breaking. When the guard dropped to the ground, Eogan followed through with a blow to the chin. He grabbed the man's weapon and dragged the unconscious soldier into the hangar.

He slammed down on the button that closed the main door.

The fewer people who saw or heard what was happening, the better.

Another guard ran up just as the door shut. Eogan seized him around the neck and choked him until he was unconscious. He dropped the soldier beside the first one, and then shot the next two men who came at him. Both of them were hit in the arm and leg. Their injuries were not life-threatening, and Eogan was able to pull them over to the others.

He used the men's handcuffs to lock them to the metal railings of the overhang doors and then he grabbed their radios. None of them had signaled for help yet, so they might be safe to continue without reinforcements. Eogan knelt down beside the first guard he'd shot and grabbed him by the collar.

"Where is the direct energy weapon?"

The man shook his head. "I don't know."

"Tell me or I will shoot you again."

"Do what you must." The man was adamant in his refusal.

Eogan pressed the muzzle of his pistol on the man's good leg and wasn't surprised to see a flicker of determination in the guard's eyes. This man would not break easily. Eogan hesitated to inflict pain on a fellow warrior who was performing his duty with honor. He had no choice. They needed the weapon and there was no time to be lost in securing it. The longer they took, the more chance there was of discovery.

A couple of seconds of silence passed as each assessed the other's resolve.

Eogan pulled back on the trigger.

"It is in a secure area beside the elevator." One of the other guards spoke up. "Wilson will never tell you."

Eogan removed his weapon. "I have no wish to kill any humans, just the Albireons."

"Be my guest." Wilson pushed away from him. "You'll never destroy them. Their power and numbers are too great."

"We will make certain they are cleared from this base." Eogan stood. "That is a start to eradicating them from Earth."

Eogan left the prisoners and went to the elevator.

Barton was waiting.

"It's in a locked storage beside the elevator."

The room was easily located. It had a large entry lock with a slide bar and keypad. Barton aimed his gun and shot. The bullet ricocheted and embedded in the wall behind them. They couldn't shoot their way through it. A code or an access card was needed to open it. Eogan glanced around the hangar and found the security computer room. There might be something there that could help them.

He went into the room and started pulling out the desk drawers. Barton followed, and was rummaging through the shelves and the storage lockers. They came up with nothing. Eogan took a step back and eased his breathing. He had to think like one of the guards. Where would they hide something as important as an access card?

In plain sight.

They used it frequently, so it had to be accessible.

He glanced around the room, past the shelves, gun racks, and computer monitors. There was a rack of hanging keys, but no access cards. Above the rack was a basket. It looked as if it was a catchall for odds and ends. He grabbed it and dumped it on the desk.

An access card was taped to the bottom.

He ripped it off and threw it at Barton.

Back at the security storage room, Barton ran the card through the slot and Eogan held his breath. He released it when he heard the soft click of the door opening.

They were in.

A racket at the hangar doors distracted them from entering the room.

"Get the weapon." Eogan started for the doors. "I'll take care of this."

He pulled his pistol out of his waistband and ran to the smaller access door. The prisoners were still handcuffed beside the sliding doors. There was another shaking of the metal and he eased his breathing before opening the door a crack. Hank Davis and his group of Resistance Fighters stood outside. Eogan pushed his door open wide.

"In here."

The group wasted no time in scurrying through the side door. The opening of the larger doors might have raised questions from someone on the base, and they couldn't risk that. Eogan locked the door after the last person was through.

It was a ragged group of men and women of varying ages. All of them armed with a gun, and ready to do battle. Eogan admired them for taking an offensive stand against the Albireons. It was no easy feat, even for him, and he was trained to do this work. The key to success was going to be coordinating their attacks.

"We have the weapon." He led Hank and the others toward the elevators.

"What about the injured guards?"

"Have someone stay above ground with them." Eogan looked behind his shoulder. "Use some of your weaker fighters to remain as lookout and to warn us of any impending change here."

Hank nodded and went back to his group. He took eight men and women aside and gave them instructions to secure the hangar at all costs. Hank knew how to command, and Eogan could only hope that his skill extended to fighting. They needed the best soldiers if they were going to defeat the Albireons.

Barton was waiting for them at the elevator.

He handed Eogan a large weapon that looked similar to a rocket launcher. "I hope you know how to use this."

Eogan had been trained on the direct-energy weapon even though it had never seen use in the field. The military had been reluctant to let the world know of its existence and that was why it had been held under a blanket of secrecy. He pushed a button on the side of its butt and the sound of a pulsing accelerator filled the air.

"This is a powerful device. Everyone must stay behind me when I'm using it. I don't want any accidental deaths." Eogan kept his voice calm. Safety precautions needed to be in place or more than the Albireons would be killed.

"We'll let you do the initial sweep of the area." Hank took a wary glance down at the weapon in Eogan's hands. "After you've finished, we'll make certain that all of the Albireons have been killed."

It was a good plan.

Real life worked differently.

Eogan hoped that Hank's past military experience was enough to complete the mission. He knew that Barton was more than capable of devising alternative options if things went wrong or he would have died in General Carter's ambush. There was no turning back now. They had to destroy the Albireons or they would be killed themselves.

The elevator doors opened.

Hank, Barton, Eogan, and ten others got on. The rest stayed behind to guard the elevator and backup those on the doors. They were prepared to join the battle if needed. Too many fighters would increase the confusion below. The last thing Eogan wanted was a disorganized attack.

Time slowed as the elevator descended. Eogan readied his weapon as the floors flashed by. So far they had the element of surprise, but if something went wrong above ground, then their escape would be blocked. He couldn't worry about that now. All he could focus on was the attack. After that, they would deal with escape.

Hank inhaled a quick breath. "Ready?"

Eogan hoisted the weapon onto his shoulder and prepared for battle. The floor clicked at level seven and the door opened.

They left the elevator and started their sweep of the Albireon quarters.

Chapter 21

Hester rubbed her arms as she watched Eogan and the others leave through the tunnel. A chill raced up her back. She hoped it wasn't a premonition of something bad. She trusted Eogan. He promised to return, and a man of honor didn't break his promises.

Unless he was captured.

She pushed the thought from her head. Eogan was a good warrior and he was fighting for a noble cause. He would come back to her. She turned away from the dark tunnel and looked at the scattering of people left behind. Most of them were women. A couple of the communication men were still here, and they had set up a radio and tracking system in the main area to monitor every move.

Lena came over. "Would you like to help with the food preparation?"

Hester nodded and followed her down one of the narrow tunnels. It was better than waiting around and worrying about what might be happening above ground. They entered an area that was no more than an alcove off the tunnel. There was a pump set up and a sink board of sorts.

"Who made the decision to make these tunnels?" The archaeologist in Hester was dying to know. "It had to be a huge endeavor."

Lena shrugged. "The original owner of this place was a survivalist. He was certain that a nuclear bomb would be dropped on the Middle East and he wanted to be prepared."

"This is a bomb shelter?" Hester could hardly believe that anyone would go to so much effort. "It must have taken him years to build it."

Lena nodded. "He spent all of his spare time down here."

"How did the H.R.F. acquire it?"

"One of our members knew the owner. The two of them were friends so when he found out that we needed a base in Turkey, he offered it."

"It's perfect. None of the tracking equipment or satellites can see you here."

"We weren't the first to think of it." Lena smiled. "Remember the underground city of Derinkuyu is in Turkey also."

"It wasn't as well equipped as here." Hester had studied pictures of the ancient underground tunnels when she was a student.

They prepared a cold meal of breads, cheeses, and fruit. They brought it into the main area for others to come and take whatever they wanted. Everyone was too anxious to think about eating, though. They picked at the food. Hester was too nervous to do anything but pace the entrance room. Back and forth she walked, trying to forget what was happening at the air base.

Surely she would sense if something had happened to Eogan.

A loud bang from the entrance tunnel reverberated around the room.

Hester stopped, and strained her ears for the sound of the men returning. Silence was all that met her. She reached out to Eogan, trying to sense if he had returned or not. Again silence. If he were in the tunnels he should be contacting her. She should hear or sense something. Their communication wasn't perfect, but she always knew when he was near.

A shiver raced up her spine.

She rubbed her arms and looked over at Lena.

"Something's wrong."

Lena nodded and then moved the others down the various tunnels. "You should hide."

Hide?

Hester was frozen in place for a few seconds as the implication of what Lena had said sunk in. It could only mean one thing. Someone from the air base was at the entrance to their hideout. It wasn't the men returning. Hester spun around and raced down the tunnel to the room that she and Eogan had originally been given. She threw the blanket over the entrance, grabbed her bag and backed into the wall beside the door.

She hugged her bag close and sank down to the floor. If the enemy had found them that could mean only one thing. Eogan had been captured. Worse, he might have been killed. Why didn't she sense that? He had said that even in death they would be connected. All she received was silence.

Was it a lie?

Were they not bonded as he said?

She shook her doubts away. Eogan was a Hunter and they did not lie. What she had experienced with him was real. Nothing could destroy the connection or the bond that they had. If Eogan wasn't responding to her it was because he was unable to. That didn't necessarily mean he was dead. He could be unconscious and hurt.

Footsteps sounded in the outer passageway.

It sounded as if a whole regiment was invading the tunnels.

Hester closed her eyes and tried to make herself smaller. She started to send out a connection to Eogan to let him know her fear and then stopped. If Eogan had been captured, the last thing he needed was to know she was in danger. Her fear would not help him. Instead, she opened her heart and sent him love. If either of them was going to die, love was the last thing she wanted to communicate.

"Well, well, what do we have here?" A deep voice spoke from her doorway.

Hester's eyes flew open.

She'd been found.

It was ridiculous to think that she could hide. Every tunnel led to rooms. All the intruders had to do was search until they found everyone. She opened her eyes to see the curtain to her room pulled back, and a large man in full military uniform was standing there. He sneered down at her. Her chin went up. She didn't know who he was, but she didn't like him.

"What do you want?"

"You." He pushed into the space and grabbed her arm. "Dr. Adams, you've sent us on a merry chase."

"I haven't done anything." Hester tried to shake the man's hand off. "You have no right to take me."

"True, but I'm going to do it just the same." The man leaned close. "Where is the Hunter?"

Hester's heart stopped for a second and then started beating frantically. She recognized the voice. He'd been talking on the phone while she and Eogan were in the elevator at the base. This was the man who'd held Eogan captive and tried to kill him. He was the enemy. She wasn't about to volunteer any information.

"I don't know what you're talking about."

"I'm not in the mood for games." The man's voice was a snarl. "You'll talk eventually. They always do."

Hester was pulled from the room and dragged down the passage until they reached the main area. Everyone else had been rounded up. Hester looked at the dejected and fearful faces of the others, and her stomach dropped. Was she the reason for this intrusion into their hideout? Had they come here because she and Eogan had sought refuge among these people?

"This is private property." Lena's voice rose above the din in the room. "Who are you and why are you here?"

"I'm General Carter." The man holding Hester spoke in a bored voice. "We have the right to do whatever we want. You're all going to the base with me."

"No." Hester shook her head. "I'm the one you want. Leave these people alone."

The general laughed. "These people are guilty of treason. Catching you was a bonus. Finding this cache of H.R.F. was our real purpose."

Hester's head felt as if it were going to explode. These soldiers were here to break up the Human Resistance Force. That could mean only one thing. They were working for the Albireons.

"You're the traitor." Hester couldn't stop herself from yelling. "You're working for aliens whose only wish is to decimate this planet. How can you stand there and let this happen?"

Carter's eyebrow rose. "They pay me well. Besides, they'll give me and my family protection."

"So you'd sellout the human race for your own skin?" Hester didn't hide her contempt.

"What's so great about humans?" The general spoke in a casual voice. "We fight and kill each other, and we'd throw our neighbor under the bus if it meant saving ourselves."

"You might do that." Hester shook her head. "I believe most people are good."

The general shrugged. "Have it your way. It doesn't make a difference. The Albireons are too strong for us to fight, so it's better to be on the winner's side rather than the losers."

"How can you sleep at night?" Hester struggled against the man who was holding her.

"Better than you will." The general motioned to his soldiers. "Round them up. I want them all transported to the base."

There was no fighting the strength of the force that had come to capture them. One by one, they were all marched to the entry of the tunnel system and pushed up the ladder. The bright headlights of open-aired transport trucks split through the night. Hester was pushed and pulled until she was forced into one of the trucks.

The others were loaded too. She clung to the side rails, and even in the darkness, she knew there was no hope for escape. Guns were pointed at them by men with cold, wooden expressions. They looked as if they'd lost the will to fight, and following orders was the only life left in them.

Lena touched her arm. "We can still hope that the others were successful."

Hester nodded. She didn't want to let Lena know that she feared the worst. No contact with Eogan and now these men were rounding them up like they were cattle. A brave face was better than dwelling on what might be their fate once the trucks reached their destination.

General Carter stood in the beam of one of the headlights with his arms crossed. The man was a monster and to think that Eogan had spent ten years imprisoned by him sent a shiver of revulsion through her. How had Eogan survived?

Just then, the general reached into his pocket and pulled out a cellphone. There was too much noise to hear what was being said, but Hester watched as the general's face went from boredom to tight anger. He'd received bad news. There was no mistaking the taut clenching of his fingers on his phone or the snap of its lid as he swirled around on his feet.

"Where is the woman?" His voice rang out above the noise.

A flashlight was shone on Hester. She blinked against the brightness that hurt her eyes.

"You think you've been clever?" The general motioned for her to be brought off the truck.

Hester was pushed through the others until she was at the edge of the truck and then she was pulled off the wooden platform and shoved at the general. His eyes were narrow and his mouth was twisted into an ugly snarl.

"You may think you've won, but I'll have the last word." The general waved up at the others still standing in the truck. "All of you thought that attacking the base was a good idea, but you're wrong. So what if you've killed a few aliens."

There was a murmur of pleasure throughout those standing on the truck. Hester felt a joy race through her too. Their mission had been a success. That was the only explanation for the general's attitude. The

H.R.F. had invaded the base and killed the Albireons that were there.

The general glared down at her. "I will have Eogan back in my control and you're going to be the one who brings him to me."

Hester shook her head. "I would never betray him."

"Knowing that I have you in my clutches will be enough." The general's lips thinned. "There's one peculiar trait that a Hunter has. They will not let a woman be hurt. All I have to do is threaten to hurt you, and he'll surrender."

"I won't let him."

The general pulled her close to him.

She could smell the sickening scent of his aftershave and her stomach rolled with nausea. This man was evil, and he'd have to kill her before she let him use her to capture Eogan.

"Round them up boys. I'll meet you back at the base."

The general kept her close as he marched her to a jeep that stood beside the two transport trucks. He reached into the front seat and pulled out a pair of handcuffs before yanking her arms behind her back and shackling her.

"We'll see who wins this game." The general muttered under his breath. "I won't be bested by an alien."

"I think that's already happened." Hester's voice was nonchalant. She wasn't going to let this man know that she was frightened.

The general pulled her up by the collar of her jacket. "He's my weapon. I know everything about him. I know what makes him tick and what buttons to push. He will be in my control by the end of this night."

Chapter 22

The electro-laser was efficient.

It burnt through the Albireon resistance with ease.

Eogan was in the lead as they swept through each room on Level Seven. The Albireons were unprepared for the attack. Eogan and the H.R.F. struck so deep in the alien nest that the Albireons had no escape options. Room by room, Eogan went in and destroyed any extraterrestrial he found.

Thankfully, this base was different from Pine Gap. No humans were being experimented on here. Instead, this was a technological center, where weapons and computers were being developed and tested. Destroying the enemy would not have gone so smoothly if they had to rescue humans also.

Hank came up beside him and shouted over the hum of the weapon-generated plasma channel. "Are they at any other levels?"

"They don't mingle with the humans." Eogan frowned. "There may be a couple who are a few levels above, but we will never get to them without injuring humans."

"So let them live?" Hank paused for a few seconds. "There's nothing we can do about that."

"You can send a couple of people up a level to check."

"It's pretty risky."

Eogan nodded. "There is one area left to clear, and then you can decided what to do next."

Eogan went to the far end of the corridor and entered the last room. It was a big meeting area and there were sleeping quarters that branched off from it. Incirlik did not hold a lot of Albireons, so the living quarters were tiny. He did a room to room search. Empty. Either they had killed all of them or they were hiding somewhere else.

"They're all dead." Hank lowered his weapon.

"We must be certain." Eogan shifted the weapon on his shoulder. It was out of charge now, but it had done a thorough job of slaying most of the Albireons they had come across. Only a few had escaped the heat of its plasma channel and those had been killed by the H.R.F.

A feeling of unease knotted his stomach. He reached out to find Hester and all that came back was fear.

He'd been so focused on the battle that he'd closed his senses to everything but the fight at hand. He was used to working alone and he was out of the habit of connecting with other Hunters during a combat. He'd lived as long as he had by sheer concentration and awareness of his surroundings. Only now did he realize that something was wrong.

"Are you in communication with the others in the tunnels?"

Hank tilted his head. "We have radio contact. Why?"

"Something is not right."

Eogan left the room and started toward the elevator.

The knot in his stomach tightened.

This time when he reached out for Hester, he connected. *"Don't come up. They've taken us and are waiting for you."*

It was a mantra that she was repeating over and over in her head. He tried to break through without success. Her fear was too great.

"They have been taken at the tunnels." Eogan ran to the elevator.

Hank followed. "How can you possibly know that?"

"Try and reach them." Eogan wasn't going to waste time explaining how he knew. He'd done what he'd set out to do and that was to kill the Albireons that were nesting in this underground base. Now he needed to do what was necessary to keep his mate safe.

Hester was a captive.

She needed rescuing.

Those were the only things that concerned him now. He pushed the button on the elevator and lowered his weapon. Hank was on a radio trying to connect with the others. He kept sending out a request. There was no return answer.

"They're not picking up." Hank looked up with a confused expression. "We're the ones who should be in danger, not them."

"It makes no difference..." Eogan didn't have a chance to finish. Just then three Albireons rushed out of one of the rooms beside Hank. They had weapons aimed at the leader of the H.R.F.

Eogan reacted.

He threw himself at the aliens, wrestling the weapon out of the hands of the first one, turning and firing it on the other two. Then he broke the neck of the one that he was holding. He threw the body to the ground and looked up at Hank.

"Are you injured?"

Hank shook his head. "Your reaction time and speed is like nothing I've ever seen before."

"This planet has benefits for Hunters."

"I'm glad of it." Hank rubbed his neck. "Thanks."

Eogan turned back to the elevator. "Make certain the floor is clear of Albireons. We need to get to the others."

There was a scuffle of activity behind him and then Hank ran back to the elevator. "The others will take care of the sweep and meet us above ground. How do you think they found the tunnels?"

"You have a traitor."

That was the only explanation that Eogan had for the breach. Nothing could be seen from above, so no satellite, or drone surveillance had spotted them. Even if they'd monitored a truck driving into the outbuildings and leaving, there should have been no reason to suspect the farm.

"Most of our members have come to us because they have had direct experience with the aliens, or they know someone who has."

"They could be lying." Eogan's voice was dry. "Humans seem very experienced with deception."

"Not all humans." Hank straightened his back. "I can personally vouch for most of the members."

"Which ones don't you know?"

"I haven't met Franklin Doan, but he's locked up here. He's never been to the tunnels."

Eogan considered the possibility that Franklin might have done surveillance on the group and rejected it. The man wasn't capable of it.

"You had met Steve Jackson also?"

"Only online. He's the one who suggested Simon and Robert. They were part of the UFO Surveillance group that he'd established a year ago."

"How long have they been with you?"

"Four months." Hank frowned. "You don't suspect them do you? Simon is outside manning the gates. If he had anything to do with this, we wouldn't have made it this far."

"That leaves Robert." A picture of the thin-faced youth came into Eogan's mind. "The last time we saw him, he was driving away from the tunnels. Did he return?"

Hank's eyes widened. "No. He should have parked the truck and hiked back to us. I was so busy with organizing the raid that I didn't notice if he returned or not."

"He isn't with us."

The elevator door opened. Eogan entered and went to stop Hank, but he pushed past and leaned against the far wall.

"If we've been betrayed, then I want to look the traitor in the eye."

Eogan understood the man's anger. It wasn't useful in battle, though. It led to mistakes, and right now if there was a contingent of soldiers waiting for them above ground, they needed all of their skills. Anger clouded both judgement and ability.

Two other men joined them before the elevator door closed.

Four against a possible army seemed like bad odds.

Eogan took a deep breath and readied himself. He'd dealt with worse before, but none of those combats had been as important as this. Hester was a captive and everything in his being wanted to roar and battle against that. He forced his breathing to a steady rhythm and pulled his assault rifle from behind his back. The direct energy weapon was useless without a charge. This would have to be done with the weapons of this planet.

The elevator stopped.

Eogan moved away from the door and pushed his back flat against the wall. The rest did the same. They all had their weapons aimed and ready to kill anyone that stopped them. The door opened with a soft ding and a blast of gunfire met them before they could exit.

Eogan crouched and started to shoot. He killed ten soldiers and Hank and his men shot the rest. A total of eighteen had been sent to meet them. Their raid on the Albireons was no longer a secret. Eogan pushed away from the door and shot another three men who were waiting. He moved for cover behind a concrete divider. Hank and the others came out of the elevator firing and rushed to the divider opposite him.

"We'll take them all down, or die trying." Hank's eyes were wide with the adrenaline rush from the skirmish. "That's the only way the others have any hope of surviving."

Eogan didn't disagree. He was more concerned about Hester. She was almost screaming in his head to run and that made no sense unless she was here and could see the battle.

"Enough." A familiar voice shouted. "You have no hope of leaving here alive."

General Carter's words sent a surge of determination through Eogan. Finally, he was in a position to fulfill his vow to destroy the man who had held him prisoner, and treated him with contempt for the past ten years. No longer was Eogan a captive. His implants had all been removed. He could not be controlled or used as a weapon.

Eogan stood up from behind the concrete divider with his rifle aimed at the general. There were at least twenty-five armed soldiers surrounding the general. They all had their weapons directed at him. Eogan's eyes narrowed. Carter might think he had the upper hand, but he was determined to see the man die.

"We have destroyed your aliens. Now it is time to kill you."

General Carter raised an eyebrow and made a waving motion behind him. "I was never very fond of the little guys. Always experimenting and ordering us around. Still, there are plenty more throughout the world. It will take more than eradicating them from one base to wipe them off the planet."

A soldier dragged a woman out of a jeep.

It was Hester.

Eogan's hands tightened around his rifle as he watched Hester being marched up to General Carter. Her eyes were pleading with him to stay put. Every nerve in his body wanted to jump at the general and throttle him. He forced his anger and disdain back. He would kill the man when the time was right. Right now, he needed to remain calm. It was the only hope he had of freeing Hester.

"I know how sensitive you Hunters are to women. Over the years, even under the pain of torture and death, that's the one thing you've refused to do. You will not harm a woman, so I've brought along your companion to help persuade you to surrender."

Eogan tightened his jaw. "You will not survive this."

"Neither will Dr. Adams." The general's voice was a sneer as he raised a pistol and put it against Hester's temple. "Drop your weapons, or the woman dies."

Chapter 23

There was no hesitation.

Eogan took a step forward.

Hester shook her head and he could feel her willing him to stop. She didn't understand that there was no choice for him. He couldn't tolerate her being held by that monster. Death was preferable to allowing anything to harm her, and Carter would make certain that she suffered. His eyes held hers as he sent her a wave of peace. He wasn't worried about putting himself in the hands of this monster again. He was asking her to trust.

Hester took a deep breath and he sensed her releasing her opposition and relaxing.

Eogan motioned behind him. "Let them go free."

"They just shot up this base." The general snorted. "I'm not about to let them waltz out of here."

"Then we have no deal." Eogan tightened his grip on the rifle.

Hester's eyes widened, and she straightened her shoulders. The soldier holding her captive, pulled her closer. Tension ripped through the hangar and for a few seconds, Eogan thought that the general was going to order an assault. Hester glanced at the pistol in the hands of the man holding her, and he knew she was planning to grab it.

Eogan willed her to stop.

She ignored him.

Carter raised his hand. "I'll let some of the people go."

Hank Davis took a step closer to Eogan. "We'll stay and fight to the last man. I won't leave Eogan here alone."

"It's your choice." The general shrugged. "I just want the Hunter. Why don't you give him to me, and you can all go free."

Hank clenched his jaw.

Eogan knew the man's sense of honor and duty rebelled at leaving another warrior behind. Eogan could handle these men. His only concern was keeping Hester safe. Hank and his men were trained fighters, but this was not their battle. They'd killed the Albireons and succeeded in their goal. This was between him and Carter. He didn't want to see anyone else injured or killed over this.

If he had to insist the others leave, then he would. Just as he was about to send the men away, words sounded in his head.

"*We are here.*"

Eogan recognized the voice of Partlan, the Hunter that he had helped escape from Pine Gap.

"*We are waiting to attack. Have your men take cover.*"

It was imperative that the H.R.F. leave the hangar before the fighting began.

"*I'm sending out the humans who helped me,*" Eogan advised through mind connect.

Eogan glanced at Hank. "You and your men must go." In a lower voice he added, "Everything is under control."

Hank gave him an intense look before nodding.

"Let them leave." Eogan waved the H.R.F. people out of the hangar. "When I know they are safe, we will talk."

The general shrugged and sent one of his soldiers to accompany the resistance fighters outside. Carter turned to Eogan.

"It's you and the girl now."

"Free her."

The general yanked Hester toward him.

She stumbled.

"*Now.*" Eogan issued the command through mind connect.

He lunged for Hester and grabbed her away from Carter. He pushed her onto the ground and covered her body with his, holding her close as the world around them exploded. Gunfire and blasts of explosives filled the air.

Eogan eased away from Hester and pushed her behind the concrete divider.

"Stay here." He grabbed his rifle. "You are safe. The other Hunters have arrived."

Her shoulders sagged.

Eogan gave her a quick kiss and then left the protection of the divider and started shooting. One by one, he took aim and killed the soldiers who surrounded the general. The other Hunters had rushed into the hangar and were attacking also. In a few minutes, all that was left was the general standing with a pistol in his hand.

"You can't touch me." Carter shouted. "My men have this place surrounded."

"Not anymore." Partlan's voice was low. "We have secured this area of the base. There will be no more killing tonight."

"It is time for you to answer for your dishonor." Eogan walked to the general. "You have used the shield of your government to cover your true activities. These are not the actions of an honorable man."

"Everyone does it."

"You sanctioned murders to further your personal interests."

"It's the way of the world." Carter waved his gun at Eogan. "You did the killing so how guilty does that make you."

"I had no choice." Eogan took another step closer to the man who had caused him so many years of pain.

"Do you think I did?"

"Yes," Eogan said. "You were in charge and made the decisions. You are the only one accountable for the consequences of your command."

At that moment, Hank Davis returned to the hangar. He glanced around at the dead soldiers and then back at the general. "As a commander, you had the responsibility to prevent deaths. You knowingly let the aliens kidnap and kill thousands of humans. That makes you a monster in my books."

"You have been judged." Eogan raised his gun.

The general shook his head. "You have no right to censure me. You're an alien."

"As a fellow officer, I have that privilege." Hank's voice was devoid of emotion. "You're guilty of gross negligence of command."

A shot rang out, and the general fell to the ground dead.

Hank lowered his gun. "It was my duty to kill him. We allowed men like him to take control, now the H.R.F. needs to make things right.

Eogan walked to the general's body. For ten years he had wanted to see this man dead and now he was. There was no satisfaction at seeing his nemesis gone. He had always thought that he would be the one to exact justice. In the end, the only thing that mattered was that the man was gone, and he could do no further harm.

Partlan walked up to him and put a hand on his shoulder. "You are free now."

Free to be a Hunter.

Eogan never dared imagine that this day would come. Words couldn't express the relief or delight he felt at knowing that he wasn't controlled and manipulated by a corrupt and dishonorable organization. It was a new existence for him. One that held hope and purpose.

"Your help was appreciated."

"You were winning. We brought the battle to a speedier end." Partlan motioned to the other Hunters with him. "This is Maloc, Gur, Ranon, and Turlo."

Just then, a beautiful blonde woman walked into the hangar. Eogan recognized her immediately. It was Grace, the woman that had been with Partlan in Pine Gap. He had helped both of them escape.

She holstered a gun and shook her head. "How come you guys always create a mess?"

Partlan held his arm out to her. "You remember Grace, my mate and wife. She is no longer with the FBI."

Hank Davis, who was standing beside Eogan, frowned. "Is it wise for you to fight with Hunters?"

"I go where my mate goes." Grace leaned against Partlan. "I have no problem killing the Albireons. They have taken control of what is not theirs, and my purpose is to eradicate them from the planet."

"We need people like you in the H.R.F." Hank's voice was full of approval.

"I'm happy that there is an organization of humans ready to take on this threat." Grace turned to Eogan. "It is good to see that you escaped Pine Gap. Partlan and I are forever in your debt for helping us. I hope they didn't treat you too badly afterwards."

"They had their suspicions." Eogan didn't elaborate. It was in the past, and with Carter dead, he could get on with the things that really mattered. He turned back to Hester and motioned for her to join them.

"This is Hester." He put his arm around her waist. "She is my mate."

Partlan nodded to Hester. "It is good to meet you."

Eogan felt Hester's trembling ease. "These are fellow Hunters who have come to help."

"Just in time." Hester straightened her shoulders. "We have to save the others from the tunnels. The general's men took them captive."

"We freed them," Partlan said. "We intercepted the convoy before it reached the base."

"Thank you. Being hostages of this organization would be brutal.

What about Franklin and Steve?" Hester's voice rose in concern. "They're still imprisoned down below."

"They are on level four." Eogan turned to Hank. "I can get them."

"My men will go." Hank motioned four of them to the elevators. "We need to take care of this area and then leave."

Eogan pulled Hester close. She'd been insane to try and help him by planning to take her guard's pistol. She could have been killed. For that brief second he had thought his own life was over. It was only the timely arrival of Partlan's team that had stopped her from carrying out her crazy plan.

He didn't want Hester to be in harm's way again. The sooner they left the area, the better. He held onto her as they began to make their way out of the hangar. Hester stopped when they came to General Carter's body.

"I'm glad he's dead. He was an evil man."

"There will be another to replace him." Eogan's voice was devoid of emotion.

Hester looked up at him. "How many replacements have you been forced to work under?"

"Too many." Eogan wanted to forget that part of his life. "The important thing is to free the others that these men have imprisoned."

"I agree." Hank crossed his arms. "I saw too many lives taken so this shadow world organization could take control of the planet. We can't let this continue."

"Ardal, our leader, has vowed that all Hunters will fight to destroy the Albireons on this planet," Partlan said. "If you are the leader of the human resistance then he will want to coordinate our efforts with you."

Hank nodded. "It makes sense to join forces. The Albireons have to be eradicated. With their demise, the human shadow organization will lose their power."

"We are working on that." Partlan turned to Eogan. "Ardal is going to meet us in London. Will it be a problem for you and your mate to go there?"

Eogan looked down at Hester and she nodded. "We'll go."

"Good. We left the helicopter at the farm where the tunnels are." Partlan turned to Hank. "Can you join us?"

Hank looked at his men and then nodded. "Yes. Barton can stay here and command the force until I return."

The elevator door pinged open.

Hank's men came out with Franklin and Steve. They looked the same as the last time he and Hester had seen them. It was obvious that neither of them had been subjected to the Albireons' questioning.

Steve smiled when he saw Eogan and Hester.

Franklin scowled.

"You left us there long enough," Franklin complained. "I thought you were supposed to be such a great warrior."

Eogan raised an eyebrow. "I could send you back."

Steve raised a conciliatory hand. "Forgive him. We are both grateful that you remembered to come back for us."

Hank went to Steve. "You must be Dr. Jackson. I'm Hank Davis. The H.R.F. has defeated the Albireons at this base with the help of Eogan and his fellow Hunters. I understand that you were thinking of joining us."

"I'm quitting." Franklin glared at Hank. "All I see are human bodies. I think it's a lie that there are any aliens. Your organization is no better than a group of terrorists."

Hank opened his mouth to speak, but Eogan stopped him. "There are no aliens here."

"I thought not." Franklin shook himself free of the men who had brought him above ground and then walked out of the hangar. No one made an effort to stop him.

"If he wanders out of the area that we've secured he will be stopped by the real military that run this base." Grace started toward the exit. "It's time we left."

Chapter 24

They were in London, England.

Hester's head was spinning at how quickly her life had changed. In less than a week, she'd gone from a lonely academic, to a woman in love. She was on the run from a shadow group of humans and aliens, who were bent on controlling and destroying the Earth. Death, guns, abduction, and terror had filled the last couple of days. Eogan had stood beside her the whole time, giving her strength and protection. If she hadn't lived through it, she wouldn't believe it.

Now, she was in a house luxurious beyond her wildest imagination.

After leaving Turkey on the helicopter, they had landed in an airport in France and then taken a jet to Heathrow. After that, a limousine had driven them to this exclusive neighborhood in Chelsea. The house was across the street from a private park. Hester wasn't very knowledgeable about the London real-estate market, but she guessed that the place cost millions of American dollars.

They were escorted into a large reception room that contained six other Hunters and a woman whose face was familiar. It took Hester a couple of seconds to remember that she'd seen her on the front pages of the tabloid papers not too long ago. She had thought that Grace was beautiful, but this woman was gorgeous. She was petite with shoulder-length dark hair and deep blue eyes that softened when they walked in.

"You made it back safely."

"Eogan had done most of the work by the time we arrived." Partlan walked further into the room. "He and the H.R.F. had killed all the Albireons. We were left with cleaning up the security detail for the restricted hangar where they were housed."

One of the other Hunters moved to stand beside the woman. "It has begun. Good."

Partlan turned to her, Eogan, and Hank Davis. "This is Darrogh, he is second in command of Ardal's unit. This is his mate, Tamsin Creighton. These are the members of his team, Savis, Firbin, Jehon, Kerm, and Breanon."

When the introductions were complete, Partlan motioned to Hank. "This is the leader of the Human Resistance Force. He has come to meet with Ardal about coordinating our attacks."

"Ardal and Catal are expected tomorrow. Tonight you should rest. You've had a difficult battle," Darrogh said.

He was right. They had slept very little in the past couple of days, and that didn't even begin to account for the stress of being on the run and fighting for their lives. The thought of sleep and the comfort of lying in Eogan's arms was hard to resist.

Darrogh walked up to Eogan. "I am glad to meet you. Your aid in saving one of our own will never be forgotten."

"A Hunter helps his brothers at all times."

Darrogh nodded. "It is good to know another member of Rioge clan lives. By Cygnus and Warrior, it will be an honor to serve with you."

Hester could sense a lightness in Eogan at the words of welcome and acceptance from the other Hunters. She leaned closer to him and he wrapped his arms around her. Comfort and love filled her.

"We'll defeat the Albireons on this planet." Eogan's voice was low with determination.

"I too have suffered at their hands. They have threatened my mate's life and I won't rest until they are all dead."

"Then we are agreed." Eogan turned to her. "This is my mate, Hester."

"You are now one of us. We welcome you, and just as we protect each other, we protect our brothers' mates."

A blanket of security and warmth had been thrown over Hester. She let herself snuggle close to the haven being offered. Darrogh's mate Tamsin came over and hugged her. She found herself being led up to a bedroom that was gorgeous enough to be featured in a home magazine.

"There's a bathroom through there where you can wash up." Tamsin pointed to an open door where Hester could see the sparkle of a crystal chandelier. "If you want to change into a dressing gown now, I'll take your clothes and put them through the washing machine. They'll be ready for you in the morning."

Hester didn't hesitate. She'd spent more time in her jeans and shirt than she cared to remember. She went into the bathroom and undressed. She wrapped the tie of the gown around her waist before going back into the bedroom and handing her clothes over to Tamsin.

"The men will probably be up late making plans." Tamsin took her dirty laundry. "I'll send Eogan up when they're finished."

"Thank you."

A thrill of excitement raced through her at the thought of spending the night alone with Eogan in this room. It was private, and the bed was large enough for both of them to get lost in. When Tamsin left, she ran her hand over the soft cream-colored cotton duvet and thoughts of getting tangled in the sheets with Eogan sent a rush of blood into her cheeks.

What did she know about tangled sheets?

The closest she'd ever come to a man was between the pages of a romance novel. It didn't matter. Tonight, she and Eogan, were going to be sleeping together, and if her body was any indication, there would be very little sleep happening. She wanted to be Eogan's mate in every sense of the word.

An hour later, after luxuriating in a large soaker tub, she snuggled deep into the sheets of the bed. She'd discarded the robe and was lying naked beneath the covers. She was humming with anticipation. When the door opened to admit Eogan, she almost squealed her delight.

Finally, he was here.

"Did you finish your plans?"

Eogan shook his head. "We'll make them tomorrow when Ardal arrives."

"You must be exhausted." Hester sat up and held the sheets close to her chest. "A shower will help."

Eogan gave her a steady look and then nodded. "I expected you to be asleep."

Hester shook her head. "I've been waiting for you. This will be the first time we have had privacy and alone time together. I want to enjoy every minute of it."

Eogan grinned. "You have plans."

Hester shrugged. "We'll discuss it after you shower."

Eogan went to the bathroom and in a couple of seconds she heard the sound of the water running. Soon, he would be with her. She was a complete novice at lovemaking, but she had waited long enough. Tonight, she was finally going to know what it felt like to make love.

Eogan came into the room several minutes later with a towel wrapped around his waist. There was a smaller towel in his other hand

and he was drying off his hair. His dark eyes never left her face as he tossed it to the side.

"What do you want me to do now?"

Hester threw back the sheets. "Come join me."

Eogan obeyed.

He let the towel drop to the floor.

Hester gasped at the spectacular vision of his naked body. He was magnificent with ripped muscles on his chest, arms, and legs. Then he walked to the bed. For the first time in her life she understood desire. Hot and heated, it raced through her. She wasn't the only one who was aroused. Eogan was massive. Her heart skipped a beat for a second when she saw the size of him. How were they ever going to fit together?

"You seem concerned."

Hester gulped and then patted the bed beside her. "We'll have to take this slowly."

"We don't have to do anything." He sat and pushed the pillows behind his back.

"I want to."

"Then you will have to guide me." Eogan turned to her. "I have never done this before."

"Neither have I." Her cheeks reddened at her admission. "No man has ever wanted me before."

"They were fools." Eogan lifted her chin with his finger. "You're an intelligent woman. Together we can figure this out."

"I know what we're supposed to do." Hester took a deep breath. "Reading something in a book, and actually doing it, are two different things."

"You know more than me." He grinned. "I've never read about mating in a book."

"Surely you've seen a movie, or something?"

"You forget where I've been for the last thirty years." Eogan's tone was wry. "Besides, there was no need for me to know. Being with a woman was forbidden."

"So what are we going to do?"

"How about we start with a kiss?" Eogan's voice was husky. "I'm sure our bodies will guide us from there."

Hester nodded. She was lost in Eogan's dark gaze as he moved closer, guiding her head so that she rested comfortably on the pillows.

He wrapped his arms around her and then his mouth was on hers, teasing and caressing until the embers of fire sparked to life. Their tongues dueled, sending shivers of delight throughout her body.

She feathered her fingers through Eogan's short-cropped hair and felt him tremble in response. A sense of power filled her as she roamed down his back, stroking and touching him until he shuddered and deepened the kiss. Her head spun and her heart raced. Within her a growing restlessness took root.

She wanted more.

Eogan ended the kiss with an exhale. "You are driving me mad."

Hester grinned. "That's the point of foreplay."

Eogan nipped her lower lip. "I can't think with you so near. All I want is to pull you close and roam my hands and lips over your body."

Hester stroked a finger across his mouth. "Your every touch is exciting me. Don't stop."

She pushed aside the covers and urged him closer.

Eogan didn't disappoint.

The trace and feel of their bodies brushing against each other, skin to skin, sent her soaring. She licked her lips and tried to calm her breathing. Eogan's eyes widened at her actions and for the first time in her life, she realized that she had power over a man.

"Kiss me." Her voice was husky with the command.

Eogan groaned and gathered her close.

"As you wish."

The world spun away, and the kiss seemed to go on forever. Eogan's hunger became hers, as together they tasted and caressed each other with their tongues and fingers. Sensations skittered across her body and she shivered with the new world of delights that had been opened for her. Never in her wildest dreams had she imagined the pleasures that Eogan was showing her.

Fevered.

Electrifying.

Thrilling.

How had she existed this long without Eogan? She craved his touch. His hands were stirring her into a frenzied, ache of longing. Her body was reaching for something as yet undiscovered, and he was the only one who could quench her thirst.

The kiss ended with both of them gasping for air. She tried to pull him back. Instead, his lips began to roam over her neck while his fingers stroked lower. She groaned as pleasure settled in her inner core. Moist heat filled her.

Until this moment, she'd never been alive.

She'd been sleepwalking through life until Eogan had awakened her.

She arched her back and urged him to continue with his exploration. His lips roamed lower, brushing against her breasts. His tongue flicked across her nipple. A piercing dart of bliss shot through her. She moaned with the exquisite delight that filled her.

Eogan lifted his head. "Did I hurt you?"

"It's wonderful." She was breathless.

Eogan grinned. "Is this what you've read about?"

"Words can't describe the ecstasy."

"Giving you pleasure is addictive."

"Then don't stop."

His fingers followed his mouth, touching and teasing until she was mindless. A craving for something she didn't understand took hold of her body. Eogan's lips and tongue moved over her abdomen and his hand roamed down her leg. She was impatient for more.

"Touch me lower." Her voice was hoarse with need.

"Show me."

Hester was beyond shyness. All thought was suspended as she floated on a cloud of feeling and sensation. She spread her legs and guided Eogan's hand higher. He brushed against her inner thighs and then rubbed her sensitive inner core.

Pleasure rippled through her body.

Eogan captured her lips as his fingers continue to tease and stroke.

Her heart raced.

Her breathing stilled.

She rode a sharp spiral of ecstasy as an intense shuddering climax shook her being. Shards of piercing bliss shot through her as the world exploded into rapture. Euphoria battled with joy.

Eogan gathered her close as she descended the heights of heaven.

She opened her eyes to see him staring down at her with concern. She gave a shaky smile and leaned up to kiss him. He'd given her such delight and still he was worried. Her love for him was overwhelming.

"Thank you."

Eogan brushed her hair from her forehead. "It was as you wished?"

"Indescribably more." Hester cleared her throat. "You were right. Our bodies would know what to do."

Eogan kissed her nose. "We have all night. I can pleasure you again if you wish."

Hester's heart skipped a beat.

She pushed him onto his back.

"There's more."

She brushed her lips against his and then trailed her mouth down his chin and neck. Her hands roamed over his chest as she tasted and licked every inch of Eogan's broad chest. It was intoxicating, and her body purred with delight. She moved lower.

Her hand stroked down the long length of his hardened penis.

He jerked in reaction.

Hester nibbled his lip. "I need your help."

Chapter 25

"Anything."

"You must promise that you won't stop."

Eogan's eyes narrowed. "I don't understand."

"A woman's first time is often painful." Hester whispered.

"I can't cause you pain."

"It is only at the beginning." Hester kissed him. "After that, it will be pleasurable."

"You are certain?"

"Trust our bodies." Hester leaned back against the pillows. "Just continue doing what you did before and everything will work out as it should."

"*I trust you.*" Eogan's voice reverberated in her thoughts.

No more words were necessary as Eogan kissed and caressed Hester until she was mindless with passion. The anticipation of their joining increased the pleasure. She was wanton in her eagerness to share the union of their bodies. Eogan might not comprehend fully what was about to happen, but he was as enthusiastic as she was.

Lips clung.

Tongues tasted and soothed.

Skin to skin, they enticed and seduced each other to a fevered passion. The world spun away until all that existed was them. Hester was riding the fine edge of the precipice again when she opened her legs and guided Eogan to her. Moist heat flooded her when she felt him at the entrance to her inner core.

She was as ready as possible.

"Now." Her voice was hoarse with desire. "Push inside."

Eogan held her hips and lifted her closer.

He thrust deep.

She inhaled a sharp breath as pain pulsed through her. It receded within seconds and was replaced with a sense of completeness. They were joined as one now. Tears sprang to her eyes as joy filled her soul.

"I've hurt you." Eogan started to pull away.

Hester clasped her legs around him. "I'm overwhelmed with the beauty of finally being joined with the man I love."

"The pain?"

"Is gone." Hester wrapped her arms around his neck and pulled him closer to her. "We were already connected by our thoughts and feelings. Our bodies are one."

The tension in Eogan's body lessened.

"You are truly my mate now."

A shiver of delight raced through Hester. She tilted her hips, drawing Eogan deeper within her, and then eased back. He mimicked her with a slow withdrawal and thrusting motion. He captured her mouth in a deep kiss where their tongues mirrored the actions of their bodies. As their hunger grew so did the pace of their lovemaking.

Hester was riding the spiral of climax again.

This time it was the movement of Eogan inside her body that was creating the coil of pleasure that tightened within her. Each thrust brought her closer to the edge until cascades of ecstasy exploded.

Eogan found his own release seconds later.

He collapsed onto her and held her close. He twisted his body, so she lay atop him as together they descended from the heights of heaven. Hester felt complete lying within Eogan's embrace. She listened as his breathing returned to normal and snuggled close. He pulled the covers over them and she yawned with exhaustion.

"Did you know such joy existed?" Eogan's voice held a note of awe.

"I think it only exists when two people are truly connected." Hester brushed her lips across his chest. "I'm glad I waited. No other man could have made me feel so wonderful."

"Can we do it again?"

Hester felt a twinge of soreness, but her desire to make love with Eogan was greater. "If we take it slowly."

"Will you still have pain?"

Hester shook her head. "I'm tender because it's new."

Eogan pulled her higher onto his chest. "There must be other ways for us to pleasure each other."

Hester giggled. "You sound like you want to try everything in one night."

Eogan grinned. "Don't you?"

She couldn't deny it.

To be held in Eogan's arms and make love was all she wanted to do. Reality would come in the morning. They had the night to explore their love and feel the magic of their bodies moving as one. They were creating memories that would last a lifetime.

"I have read about different ways of making love." Hester lowered her voice. "There is one way in particular I found very intriguing."

"Tell me."

"We use our mouths and tongues to excite each other."

Eogan's body tensed.

Hester grinned. "After that, who knows what will happen."

Eogan twisted their bodies until she was beneath him. His lips captured hers and within seconds the passion and desire that was just below the surface, ignited again. Together, they began to explore and pleasure each other until exhaustion and sleep claimed them.

Light was filtering into the room when Hester awakened.

She blinked the sleep from her eyes as she left the last remnants of the best dream she'd ever had. She'd been held by a man who loved her to distraction. It had been beautiful, and she hadn't wanted to wake. She groaned and stretched her arms over her head.

"Are you in pain?" Eogan's voice was laced with concern.

It wasn't a dream.

Hester reached up and ran a finger down Eogan's cheek. He had been so gentle with her last night that it had almost brought tears to her eyes. This man who was so strong that he could kill with his bare hands, had held her like she was the most fragile piece of china. Her heart was filled to bursting with love.

"I feel perfect."

The concern left Eogan's eyes. He leaned down and kissed her until the fires that had burned deep into the night started to stir. His tongue twirled with hers and for several moments all thought was gone as Hester surrendered to Eogan's touch.

He ended the kiss when they were both gasping for air.

"Enough. You are sore and we need to talk."

Regret filled her.

Eogan was right. She ached in places she never knew existed before. They'd made love several times last night, and as much as she wanted to feel him deep inside her again, she was too tender. Soon, she would be ready again. Until then, they still had plans to make about their future.

She fluffed up her pillows and leaned back against them. "What concerns you?"

"You." Eogan pulled her close. "I need to continue working with the other Hunters to defeat the Albireons, but I'm worried about your safety."

A knot formed in her stomach. Was this where he told her they had to separate for her own good? What if something happened to him, or he never came back? She couldn't handle having touched paradise and then never to see it again.

"I could go back to work at the university."

"I will always desire to have you with me," Eogan said in a fierce voice. "I can't focus on doing battle if I'm concerned about your safety."

"Are you certain that you don't want to be rid of me?" Hester couldn't hide her insecurity.

"You are my mate. A Hunter mates for life. I would die if something happened to you." Eogan brushed his lips across the top of her head. "It is no longer safe for you at the university. I think you should stay at the compound that the other Hunters have set up."

Hester frowned. "Where is that?"

"It's in a remote area of Canada." Eogan stroked a hand down her arm. "That is where the other mates are staying. We are concerned that the Albireons will be more vigilant in their attempts to stop us."

"That only stands to reason." Hester pulled away and looked up at Eogan. "You're killing them. If they don't fight back, they'll be dead."

"Hunters battle with honor. The Albireons have never been known for fighting a just combat. They will use whatever techniques they can."

"You think they'll kidnap me?"

"You and the other wives." Eogan's voice was serious. "This was why it was forbidden for a Hunter to mate. Our bond is strong because of all the genetic modifications that have been done to us. We will do anything to defend our mates."

"So they'll use me against you, just like General Carter did."

Eogan nodded. "Carter didn't realize that we were bonded, or even the significance of that. All he knew, was that Hunters are bound by the Sacred Code to protect women and children at all costs."

"He got lucky." A shiver went through Hester as she considered what horrible things the general might have done if he'd known about a Hunter's pair bond.

"It is well he didn't know."

"Reading my thoughts again?" Hester smiled up at him. A glow of happiness flowed through her at the uniqueness of their bond. Last night had taken it to a new level, and she knew that as time went by, it would only grow stronger.

"We are one. Your thoughts, feelings, and fears are mine."

Hester stretched up and gave Eogan a quick kiss. "What am I thinking now?"

A fire sparked in Eogan's dark eyes, followed by a shadow of regret. "It would be my pleasure at any other time. We need to discuss your future."

"I'll go where you decide." She didn't want to give up her post at the university. She'd worked too hard to earn her position. "I can ask for a leave of absence until this problem is solved."

"We will defeat the Albireons soon. Then, I will live with you at your university."

"Really?" Joy filled her at the thought of Eogan joining her. "Most men want to pursue their own careers."

"I only want to be with you. You enjoy your work and when you are happy, so am I." Eogan's voice was sincere. "You'll want to continue your research and I will go with you."

"What about fighting?"

"I have not decided yet. Most Hunters my age are dead." Eogan's voice sounded weary. "I have spent thirty years following the orders of others. Now I need to consider what I will do."

"Will you join with the other Hunters?"

"We are brothers. I will always be available for them."

"Then that is settled." Hester jumped out of bed and grabbed Eogan's arm. "I will go where you want me to until the Albireons are defeated. After that, together we'll decided where to live. You'll have a better idea of what you want to do by then. If not, my teaching can support both of us."

Eogan stood. "It is time to get dressed."

Hester pulled him toward the washroom. "After we shower."

The next hour was filled with steam, caresses, and kisses until Hester was out of her mind with need. Only then, did Eogan give in to her pleas, and make love to her. It was sensual and fulfilling, and even though she still had a few twinges of pain, the pleasure far outweighed any of her aches.

When they were finally dressed, Hester gave Eogan a hug. "I love you."

"You are with me always." Eogan's voice was low.

"You are the only man that has truly seen me."

Hester didn't know how to tell Eogan what he'd done for her. She was confident and assured in her academic pursuits, but never in her personal life. For the first time, she felt beautiful. Bonding with Eogan had done this for her. She needed to express what was in her heart.

"There is no need for words." Eogan lifted her chin. "We are connected in every sense."

Hester blinked back her tears of joy. "I don't want you to ever doubt my love. You make my heart soar."

Eogan brushed his lips across her mouth. "Our connection is growing stronger."

There was a knock at the door.

"Ardal and Catal have arrived."

Chapter 26

Two Hunters stood when Eogan and Hester entered the reception room.

Eogan recognized Ardal immediately.

The second Hunter had a grim expression on his face. There was an instant mind connect. *"Do you forgive me?"*

It was Catal.

He had not seen the man since they were both incarcerated by the humans after their ship crashed on Earth. Catal had been a boy of ten, and Eogan had helped him escape. A rush of relief went through him. Catal had grown strong and well.

Eogan went up to the Hunter. "By Cygnus and Warrior, it is wonderful to see you alive."

"I feared you would never speak to me again. I abandoned you."

"You were free. That was my only concern."

"When you were silent, the others thought that you were dead. That's why we didn't come back and rescue you." Catal's voice was filled with regret.

"Our communication was blocked. How many survived?"

"Less than fifty are still alive." Catal glanced over at Ardal. "Ardal finished our training and has taken command of all the Hunters on the planet."

A weight was lifted from Eogan.

He had carried the guilt and blame for the loss of lives on the ship for years. Worse, he'd been told lies that had led him to believe that he was the only Hunter who had survived. He'd only been fifteen when they had crashed. It had been his first mission alone, but because he was clan Rioge, he was the leader and responsible for the others.

He turned to Ardal. "It is an honor to meet in person."

"The honor is mine." Ardal and he were the same height and build. "You and I are the only two left of Clan Rioge."

"I hear there is one other."

Ardal frowned. "Is another held prisoner?"

"I am speaking of your daughter."

Ardal grinned. "I hadn't thought of that. You are right. She is Clan Rioge. It is a first to have a woman of Hunter blood. You are aware that Catal has a son too."

"It is good that the old legends are true." Eogan motioned for Hester to join him. "I have also found my mate. This is Hester Adams. She is an archaeologist who has been studying the ancient anomalies on this planet."

Ardal gave her a slight bow of the head. "It is a pleasure to have another woman amongst us. My wife, Fiona, will be delighted to meet you."

"Thank you."

Hester clasped Eogan's hand and a surge of pride raced through him. She was claiming him as her mate in front of his fellow warriors. It was truly an honor to have such a woman beside him. She was courageous and intelligent. Her curiosity and determination to find the truth, had led her across the world. If she hadn't followed her intuition, he would never have found her. He was indeed a lucky man.

"I hear you have a compound where it is safe to stay."

Ardal nodded. "Until we have dealt with the Albireons, all Hunters and their mates must be on guard. Darrogh and his mate, Tamsin, are staying in London with a full team because the work they are doing here is vital for the fight against the Albireons.

Someone cleared their throat behind them.

Eogan motioned Hank Davis forward. "This is Hank. He was a former soldier with the Albirsion Corporation. When he saw what was happening to abductees, he escaped and formed the Human Resistance Force. His team helped me kill the Albireons in Incirlik."

"A very brave man." Ardal's voice held approval. "You wish to coordinate with us in defeating the Albireons?"

"It makes sense that we should work together." Hank crossed his arms. "I have people all over the world who are waiting for me to give the command to attack. They believe that there is hope to rid the Earth of this scourge."

"They have been on this planet for over seventy years. It will not be easy."

"What other option do we have?" Hank's voice was filled with scorn. "Are you afraid?"

"A Hunter has no fear." Ardal's eyes narrowed.

The other Hunters crossed their arms.

Eogan took a step closer to Ardal.

"We are not your enemy," Eogan said in a firm tone.

Silence followed his words.

Hank glanced between the two men. "I have offended you. I apologize."

"We have been fighting Albireons long before they came to this planet. Many of my brothers have experienced pain and torture at their hands." Ardal relaxed his stance. "We have taken steps to defeat them."

"We are in control of their finances." Darrogh who had been standing beside Tamsin Creighton, spoke. "In a few months, Savis should be able to unlock all of their computer systems and destroy them from within."

"We still require fighters on the ground. We need to hunt and abolish them where they are hiding." Ardal glanced at Hank. "Are your people prepared to do whatever it takes?"

"It is our only choice." Hank grimaced. "We can't allow them to continue living on Earth."

"There can be no second guessing our methods." Ardal's voice was stern. "The extent of the Albireon infiltration on this planet requires quick and decisive action."

"Understood."

"Then we will join forces with you." Ardal held his hand out to Hank.

Eogan's tension eased as he watched the men shake hands. The pact was sealed. With Hunters and humans working together there was a good chance they would be able to defeat the Albireon threat. This was the opportunity he'd been waiting for since his capture, to destroy those that had imprisoned him. He had been lied to and kept away from his fellow Hunters. He could not forget that. There was no honor in the Albireons' actions, only greed.

"It would be best to hit the major bases at the same time. I am familiar with Pine Gap and I know of several facilities in the United States," Eogan said.

"I was stationed at Dulce Base. It was what I saw there that convinced me the aliens had to be obliterated from our planet." Hank Davis's voice held a note of anger. "I have people in the H.R.F. who have been in all the various underground bases throughout the world. They will give us the intelligence we need to attack."

"Good." Ardal nodded. "We will devise a plan to coordinate our efforts."

"We have enough funds from our years as hired mercenaries to launch a full scale war." Catal's voice was rueful. "That should be enough to outfit us."

"I will contribute as well." Everyone turned when Tamsin Creighton spoke. "I do have a very large trust fund. My father will probably help too."

"This is more than I could ever have hoped for." Hank rubbed a hand over his face. "With this much help and resources we should be able to take the planet back and make certain the Albireons no longer threaten humans."

"The attacks have to be a surprise and multi-pronged," Ardal said. "With the proper timing we can storm all their defenses at the same time."

"So it is decided that we attack the Albireons as one." Eogan's voice was low with determination. "It will be good to see them crushed."

Ardal nodded. "You will be in control of the European and Australian forces. I will deal with the North and South American threats. We will work together on the rest of the bases."

Eogan felt purpose surge through him. He was clan Rioge and bred to be in command. Training and genetics had made them leaders. Eogan had spent over thirty years in isolation, but he could not hide his breeding. He was born to lead, and that was what he would be doing now.

Ardal turned to Darrogh. "We need to discuss this further. Is there a place to sit and plan?"

Darrogh grinned. "This house has many such places. I prefer the kitchen."

"Good. We could also use a meal."

Tamsin jumped up. "You must be starved. Let me get some breakfast ready."

"I'll help." Hester released Eogan's hand and followed Tamsin from the room.

Grace and Partlan also went to the kitchen, along with Darrogh and Ardal. Hank was quick to follow.

Eogan moved to go when a hand on his shoulder stopped him. He turned to see Catal.

"It's good that you have found a mate." Catal's voice was warm. "I mistrusted what I was feeling when I found my mate, Selena, and that cost me eight years of regret. I'm glad you were able to recognize what was happening to you."

"I had the benefit of meeting Partlan and Grace. Still, it was a shock. I had just removed my implants so I couldn't be certain if it was real."

"You sacrificed your life so that I could be free. There is no way that I can repay you. It would be an honor if you would let me join your team in this battle."

Eogan was humbled by Catal's words and loyalty.

"The honor is mine." Eogan and Catal started for the kitchen. "It is no sacrifice to rescue a fellow brother. Together, we will fight those who have done harm to us and this planet."

As they walked into the kitchen, Eogan saw Hester putting plates on the table and he went to help. When he'd been told that all the other children who had crashed with him were dead he'd been consumed with desolation and loneliness. Over the years, his isolation had robbed him of the sense of purpose that being a Hunter gave him. He had thought it was a long-lost memory.

Today he remembered.

He was part of a brotherhood of warriors once again.

True happiness came from finding his mate, Hester. Last night in her arms he'd touched paradise. Her acceptance and love completed him. She was the most important person in his life and the thought of losing her was unbearable. He would fight to destroy the Albireons and make the world safe for her.

All his years of imprisonment faded as he considered the life ahead of him with Hester. The future held hope and love. He had purpose and a place with his fellow Hunters. He was no longer dead to them or forgotten.

He was finally home.

THE END

Thank You

Thank you for reading aHunter4Gotten. I hope you enjoyed Eogan and Hester's journey.

If you liked aHunter4Gotten, please consider leaving a review.

If you would like to know when my next book is released, sign up for my newsletter at
www.cynthiaclement.com/contact

To get further information about my books visit my website at:
www.cynthiaclement.com

Author's Note

Gobekli Tepe was first discovered in 1963 by an American archaeological team. At that time, it was labeled a Neolithic site and considered not to have any real importance. It wasn't until the German archaeologist, Klaus Schmidt, began excavations in 1994 that the true significance of the site became apparent. It is located seven miles northeast of Sanliurfa, Turkey, and consists of several layers of occupation, with the oldest dating from approximately 9,600 BCE.

Less than 5% of the area has been uncovered. What has been found are stone circles of large T-shaped pillars with elaborate carvings of animals and stylized symbolic beings. There is evidence of ritual usage, but as of yet, nothing to suggest that people occupied the structures. That is why it is said to be the world's oldest temple.

Its existence is changing our understanding of pre-history man and their capabilities. It appears that man did not need a sedentary life-style of farming to build temples. Hunter-gatherers were building also, and this site suggests that settlements may have occurred after the temples were built.

Another interesting fact about Gobekli Tepe is that the whole area was deliberately covered up. Who would do this and why would it have been necessary?

Other questions are raised about the purpose and use of this site.

Why were predators depicted on the stone pillars?

What was the area used for... ritual or communal living?

Why build in circles?

Geophysical surveys suggest that there are still at least twenty more circles buried at the site, so that means the shape of a circle had significance. Considering the large number of later-dated stone circles built around the world, this significance carried over to other cultures and civilizations.

Some alternative history followers have suggested that because of the age of this site, and its location, that it is the original Garden of Eden mentioned in the Bible. The area would have been filled with forests and wildlife at the time it was built, so it might have seemed to be a paradise.

There is no doubt that the site is fascinating, and the artistry used on the pillars superb. If hunter-gatherers were responsible for building these structures, their talent and skills have been underestimated. It took knowledge of building permanent structures that could survive centuries to construct these monoliths, and to carve and sculpt such beauty with stone and bone tools is truly magnificent.

Unfortunately, we will never be able to discover the true reason or necessity for creating such an elaborate site. No written documentation has been left so we are left to conjectures that encompass the mundane and the fantastic. This speculation is what fascinates me. Why do you think so many stone circles were built? What was their purpose and meaning?

About the Author

Cynthia Clement is an award winning and bestselling author who began writing stories in her teens, but it wasn't until her forties that she became serious about writing. She believes in second chances, exploring new ideas, and bringing the impossible to life. Her novels, whether contemporary, historical, or science fiction, all focus on love, honor, and intrigue.

She lives in Canada with her husband of thirty-three years, her teenaged son, and two dachshunds. She has an eclectic range of interests including paranormal phenomena, ghost hunting, quilting, reading, gardening, and great conversation.

Her first book, The Seduction of Sarah, was a finalist in the HOLT Medallion Best First Book Category. Her book, aHunter4Rescue, has placed first in the 2014 International Digital Awards in the Paranormal Category and received third place in the 2014 ACRA Heart of Excellence Reader's Choice Award, Paranormal Romance Category

Books Available

Science Fiction
aHunter4Hire series

aHunter4Rescue
aHunter4Saken
aHunter4Life
aHunter4Ever
aHunter4Trust
aHunter4Gotten
aHunter4Fire
aHunter4Right

Historical
Caldern Family

The Seduction of Sarah
The Seduction of Madalyn

Novellas
Pleasuring Emily
Christmas Kisses
Christmas Loves

Contemporary
Wednesday Wives Club

www.ingramcontent.com/pod-product-compliance
Lightning Source LLC
Chambersburg PA
CBHW031350170626
46807CB00002B/910